BOOK THREE IN THE *DARKNESS* TRILOGY

THE

AWAKENING

REBECCA HAMBY

Dedicated to

My incredible readers, this one's for you.

PLAYLIST

The Summoning – Sleep Token
Pain – Three Days Grace
Morally Grey – April Jai
Like a Villain – Bad Omens
Voices in my Head – Falling in Reverse
Another Life – Motionless in White
Limits – Bad Omens
This is War – Thirty Seconds to Mars
Give em Hell – Everybody Loves an Outlaw
Awake Alive – Skillet

CHAPTER 1

SLOAN

My lungs burn every time I inhale a breath. Every muscle fiber in my body screams, telling me to slow down, but I can't. I can't stop running now, or he'll surely catch me. Running through the dense, wet forest, I try to stay light on my feet. I quickly jump over piles of leaves and dodge the tree limbs that litter the muddy ground. The air is painfully cold; the wind biting into my skin through the thin, long-sleeved top that's hugging my skin. My jeans are already soaked, causing my legs to stiffen from the frigid air, making running harder.

It's late October. Summer has come and gone too quickly, and I'm left wishing for the sun's warmth with each passing day. Continuing to run, I spot a large tree with a wide trunk at its base. I sprint towards it, hoping to conceal myself to catch my breath. Grabbing the tree's trunk, I spin my body around, pressing my back against the freezing wet bark as I try to control my breathing. Keeping still, I close my eyes and focus on what I hear. I don't dare peek around to see and risk exposing my hiding spot. I hear the slight rustling of the trees against the wind, but what I'm listening for is him, but I can't hear him.

I stay in this spot for a moment longer. Once my breathing has calmed, I sprint once more, pushing off the tree's roots and digging my heels into the Earth. When I see the opening of the forest and a beam of light becomes visible through the tree line, I smile in satisfaction. I've made it. I'm almost there. I'm about to reach the outskirts of the forest, when I'm thrown to the forest ground. A heavy mass collides with my back, pinning me against the freezing mud. I thrash and fight, gathering all my strength to roll beneath him and free my body. Using my legs, I can maneuver half my body sideways, allowing me to move and come out on top of my attacker. Pulling my knife from the strap that's secured above my boot, I push the blade to the throat of my attacker. He stops moving, raising his hands in a silent surrender.

"You stopped running. You gave the enemy time to catch up with you. Never give them that chance." Arno's breathing heavily as I straddle his waist, still pressing my knife to his throat.

"Does it matter? Do you see where you are now? It

looks to me like I've won." My smile is wicked as I lower my face to his.

I'm about to ease my blade away from his throat, but he grabs my wrists in his large hands. He lifts my body up and over his head with his legs, causing me to land flat on my back. The air is instantly knocked from my lungs, and I struggle to suck in a breath. I close my eyes and wince at the pain, but the sound of a gun cocking has my eyes shooting open.

"Cockiness will get you killed, little one. Besides, never expect to win a gunfight with a knife." With that, Arno reaches out his hand to mine. I willingly grab his as he pulls me to my feet in one swift motion. It takes me a moment to catch my breath as I re-sheathe my blade, and Arno places his gun back in the holster.

I've been training to become a Shadow now for six months. Every day is different—from weapons training to technology to hand-to-hand combat to days like today. Today is Arno's day of training, and we've been focusing on the art of escaping without being captured. He's explained that on some jobs, once the target has been eliminated, I will be left exposed. Thus, forcing me to flee the location unde-tected—easier said than done. We've been running this lesson most of the morning. I eliminate said target and then proceed to try to make my escape towards the end of the forest, which is lining the edge of The Shadows' Headquarters.

I have yet to make it successfully to the opening, and my frustration is now at an all-time high.

"Why can't I simply kill anyone who chases me?" I could have easily killed Arno and won this match, so why can't I protect myself and kill anyone who follows me? They wouldn't be good people if they had communicated with the target.

"Sloan, I've told you this before. You kill the target and no one else. Unless they're an active threat, meaning they are actively trying to kill you. Other than that, they're off limits."

I scoff as we both turn and start walking back towards headquarters.

"Well, that's plain stupid. If they are chasing me, isn't that a threat?" I complain as my teeth start chattering from the cold.

"Okay, let's say you do kill everyone. Who's to say you didn't kill someone of high importance?"

"Example?" I ask, drawing out the word in annoyance. He doesn't answer me immediately, but another voice appears ahead, answering for him.

"Let's say you kill an innocent politician who is working towards ending sex trafficking. A woman who's simply in the wrong place at the wrong time. Maybe a girl who is walking home from a busy day working at the coffee shop." I lower my head, absorbing his words. He's right; I can't become so dissociated that I no longer care about killing people. I need to be mindful. I need to be one step ahead. Everett's frame comes into view. He's walking towards us, maneuvering through the trees in and out of sight.

Arno and I both stop, waiting for Everett to reach us. When he does, he leans down to kiss my forehead before speaking again. "We only kill those who deserve to be killed. We kill because, without those people, the world is a better place. Killing just to kill is what makes them different from us. We kill with a purpose and intention." He's gazed down at me, his green eyes fixated on mine as he pulls me in for a hug.

"You're fucking freezing. Let's get you inside." I nod, thanking the heavens he's here. I think I might die from hyperthermia if I'm out here any longer. Everett wraps his arm around my shoulder, pulling me tightly to his side as we approach the building. Arno comes to my other side, walking in sync with us.

"I have to say, mate, she's getting faster and a lot fucking stronger." He wraps his hand around his throat before continuing, "She almost slit my throat a moment ago." Arno snickered. I glanced to Everett for his reaction, his crooked smile pulling on his cheek as he lets out a laugh. The satisfaction Everett gets whenever he hears about me hurting or attempting to kill Arno is that of a proud boyfriend.

Everett glances down at me, giving me a wink, a sudden sense of pride filling my chest. It's been over a year now that I've been with my guys. A year since they kidnapped me off the streets, brought me to

Stone Fortress, then came back and saved me from that sex trafficking shit show. I still can't believe this is the life I'm living.

We continue walking along the forest as I listen to Arno and Everett talk about my training. They both agree I'm excelling in hand-to-hand combat, weapon skills, and building my strength. I'm not, however, excelling in technology. Computers have never been something I've been intelligent with. Hacking and coding are such a foreign language to me; I just can't grasp the concept. Arno says it'll take time and practice, but I still can't imagine being able to understand how ones and zeros can be used to communicate. Numbers are not letters in my mind, and I pray it'll all make sense to me soon.

We reach the end of the forest and make our way out of the cover of the trees. The cool air bites my skin as the trees no longer provide some protection from the icy wind. I glance to my right, and the familiar ache in my chest begins as I see Colson's grave nestled in the corner of The Shadows' personal cemetery. It lies in a small meadow before the forest starts, blocked off by a beautifully ornate black iron fence that wraps around the land. It still hasn't gotten easier to see his resting place. The pain is still there, and I fear it will never go away. As if he, too, feels the pain of losing his brother every time he sees his tombstone, Everett squeezes my hand a bit tighter.

"I miss him too, love. He'd be so proud of you," his voice is low, but Arno and I both hear him. I hold back the familiar sting of tears building behind my eyes. I'm about to say something back, but Arno beats me to it.

"He's laughing in his grave right now at how much of a beating you've put me through this past week. I can hear his smug ass now." He changes his voice to sound less deep and more Colson-like. "Slice his throat sweetheart, no one will miss his arrogant ass." I laugh at Arno's attempt at sounding like Colson, and I hear Everett try to hold back his laugh but fail. Arno has kept us laughing as Everett, Dean, and I mourn Colson's loss. They say time heals all wounds, but that's a damn lie. No length of time will heal the pain of losing a piece of my heart, a fragment of my soul.

CHAPTER 2

SLOAN

We reach headquarters, and the moment we step through the doors, warmth engulfs my frozen body as I slowly begin to thaw. The three of us continue down the hall until we reach the locker rooms.

"Go take a shower, love, and warm up. Meet us back in the lounge when you're done, and we'll go over the rest of the week's training plan," Everett says before leaning in and kissing me gently. He and Arno continue down the hall, leaving me alone.

Heading into the locker room, I head straight to one of the three showers located at the back and immediately turn the faucet to a scalding temperature. I head to my locker and begin stripping off my wet clothes, discarding them at my feet. This isn't a high school locker room, instead, it's more of a spa-like atmosphere. Not that I've ever been to a spa before to compare, but this is what I imagine a resort to resemble. The small room with the lockers is carpeted in a deep red color, and each locker is made of dark wood and is large and spacious. Your fingerprint is your key to open your locker. I couldn't be happier that I didn't have to remember a number lock or hold a key that I would surely lose.

It's serene in here, the only noise is the spray of the running shower. Stripping down until I'm entirely naked, I grab my towel and go to the shower. It's now wholly blanketed with steam, and I can hardly see in front of me as I continue walking mindlessly through the tiled room. When I know I'm standing in front of my shower. I hang my towel and open the glass door, allowing the steam to billow. The warm mist is soothing as it seeps into my bones and warms me from the inside out.

Stepping into the shower, the water is boiling I have to step back and modify the temperature. I'm waiting for the water to cool down, testing the spray with my hand, when I hear the faint sound of the locker room door clicking shut. I turn to see who it could be, but after a few moments, I hear nothing.

"Hello?" My voice echoes off the walls as I wait for a response. Nothing.

"Hello, someone there?" I ask, but again, there is no answer. I grab my towel, wrap it around my body, and close the shower door, leaving the water running. Walking slowly, I reach the corner of the small hallway that separates the lockers and the shower room. I expect to see someone fiddling with their locker, but the small room is shockingly empty. I stand there momentarily, waiting to hear anything more, such as the toilet flushing or the sink turning on. When I hear nothing, I turn back around to head to the shower again. Perhaps I was hearing things.

Since being thrown into this unpredictable and chaotic lifestyle, I've become jumpier and aware of the slightest noises, so much so, I feel like my mind plays tricks on me. I reach the shower and remove my towel once again. Cracking the glass door a bit, I test the water temperature to find it has reached an optimal heat. I open the door fully to step in completely. Just before I do, a rigid body wraps around me from behind, holding my arms tight to my body.

My instincts kick in, and I begin to fight back. I drop my body, allowing my total weight to buckle beneath me. I hoped this move would've allowed me to slip from their grasp, but I quickly realized this person was much stronger than I gave them credit for. My body hardly budges. They squeeze me harder as my legs connect with the floor again.

I fight and swing my head back, trying to connect with their face, but I'm hitting nothing but air. Weighing my options, I viciously kick backward, connecting with their legs but doing little to harm them. This person is massive and built like a fucking boulder.

"Get the fuck off me!" I scream, my voice echoing

through the locker. I've been told not to waste my energy on talking or screaming, but now, I'm so frustrated I can't help myself. Suddenly, I'm being pushed into the shower as the water sprays down on my face. My body is pressed hard against the tile wall, and whoever is behind me lays their body flush against my backside. My breathing is heavy as I lift my leg in front of me to try to push myself off the wall. I get one leg up, readying to move our bodies back, when a familiar voice fills my ear.

"You're turning into quite a fighter, baby girl." His deep voice fills my head as his lips brush against my ear. My body begins to relax as his arms slowly start to ease their hold on me. I don't turn around right away; I savor the feeling of his lips on my wet skin. His mouth wanders down my neck until he stops on the top of my shoulder. He lingers there for a while kissing at my cigar-burn scar as if he can magically kiss away the imperfection.

"You know it's not nice to sneak up on a woman. Especially when she's naked," I say over my shoulder, our cheeks brushing together as he continues to kiss my scar ever so lightly. He pulls away, allowing me to turn around to meet his gaze. Dean is standing completely naked, the water cascading down his muscular frame. My eyes follow the water spray as it dips and glides down each of his glorious muscles.

"You're in training. This was simply another test." His voice is full of mischief as the corner of his mouth lifts slightly, giving me a devilish smirk. I take a small step towards him, our bodies centimeters from touching.

"Did I pass?" I look up to his face, carefully avoiding the water so it doesn't pelt my face. Dean raises his hand to the side of my neck, pulling his bottom lip into his mouth as he lowers his face to meet mine.

"You failed." His lips crash onto mine before I even have the chance to argue with him. I want to fight against his hold on my neck, but Dean has a way of making me surrender to his touch. My body instantly betrays me as I kiss him back with equal ferocity. I wrap my hands around his neck and pull him deeper into the shower until my back is pressed up against the tile once more. His hard length grows against my stomach as our tongues start to fight one another. I let out a soft moan against his lips as he tilts his hips, grinding harder into me. Instinctively, I wrap my legs around his slim waist, continuing to hold his neck, not once separating our mouths from one another. We are hungry, devouring each others lips as if this is our last meal.

The moment we lost Colson was the moment we started living life as if each moment was our last. I'll never take for granted time with either of my men. Every day, every hour, every minute is cherished and spent like it'll be our last. Everything feels as though it's been heightened. My emotions are stronger, and my sense of smell, sight, and touch have been strengthened to new levels. People say when you lose a sense, the other senses become greater. I can attest to that. This was true for me when it came to losing Colson. I lost one of my senses, and everything within me has now been amplified.

Dean's hands are butter gliding across my wet body, exploring every curve, every scar, and all my sensitive spots that only Dean and Everett have yet to find. Dean's grasp on my body is rough, not painful at all, but hard enough for me to know I am his. I belong to him—a part of me will forever belong to him.

He reluctantly pulls away from my lips, breathing heavily as he tries to catch his breath. Leaning his forehead against mine, he presses his body into me, his hands gripping my ass, squeezing me hard enough to leave handprints.

"I'll never get enough of you. You're my oxygen, and I can't catch my breath." Dean's voice is low, his lips brushing mine as he speaks. He claims my mouth with his once again as he lines himself up at my entrance.

"Kidnapping you was the best thing I've ever done, and I'd do it all over again." He doesn't let me respond. He thrusts into me once, fully seating himself, making me gasp. The sudden pain subsides as my body begins stretching for him. He stays fully buried inside me for a moment before pulling out slowly and thrusting harder and deeper inside me once more.

"Fuck, baby girl, your pussy is perfection." His moans fill the small space, bouncing off the tile walls as he begins to thrust faster. My back slaps against the tile wall with each motion. Dean snakes his hand between us, quickly finding my clit and making circular motions—fast and fluid. It takes no time for me to feel the crest of an orgasm building within my core. My abdominal muscles flex as his fingers work me like a piano, his cock starting to twitch inside me. He's close, his speed picking up once more. Our breathing is erratic and wild. Two feral beings devouring one another. Two hungry wolves fighting each other for the release we both search for.

My walls begin to tighten around him as my orgasm rushes through me like a tsunami, quickly breaking me down from the inside, and causing me to see stars. My pleasure soars through me, creeping into every crevice of my being. My fingers, my toes, my brain, everything feels as if I'm drunk. I'm drunk on Dean. I never want this sensation to stop. My internal temperature is at a million degrees as my orgasm sparks fire beneath my skin. Dean suddenly stops thrusting as he finds his own release, his pleasure spilling inside me. Our bodies fuse together as one; not a single part of my body is without a piece of Dean as he presses himself firmly into me. Our breathing becomes synced as we slowly come down from our euphoric pleasures.

He curls his hands around my face gently and brings his lips to mine. Kissing me softly, he slowly slips out of me, the sudden emptiness causing me to moan against his mouth. Kissing me gentle and slow, the sensual side of Dean emerges as his inner beast finds its hiding spot once more. Until next time.

CHAPTER 3

SLOAN

After we shower, Dean and I head to the lounge to join Everett and Arno. Walking into the lounge together, freshly showered and freshly fucked, Everett gives us a knowing look along with his signature crooked smile.

"Took you both long enough. I debated coming to find you." Everett's voice is playful as he scans me up and down before shooting me a subtle wink.

"I was going to come look for you, but this bloke threatened my life if I did," Arno said, leaning back into his lounge chair. His large frame spread across the chair; his legs opened wide. His smile was all mischief as he gave Dean a taunting look. I didn't miss Dean's low growl at his statement, the protective beast trying to make his escape.

"I'd have to say that would've been a stupid mistake, Arno. I know you're smarter than that," I joke with him as I make my way over to Everett's side, taking up the empty seat beside him on the large couch.

"Yeah, you're probably right, little one, plus I'm finally in their good graces. Don't want to fuck that up, now do I?" Arno replied to me as if Dean and Everett weren't in the room with us. I shoot him a smile, this new friendship with him is turning into something I never thought I would need.

From starting off as a total prick, to becoming this, whatever this is. I like him, and I need this friendship more than I realized. He believes in me; he sees something in me that no one has seen until now. Arno trusts me. He doesn't treat me like some glass doll that will break at any moment. To Arno, I'm one of the guys, a 'bro-girl', as he likes to call me.

I went from feeling like a burden to being included in this society—in this crazy-ass world of chaos. This is the new me; I've felt reborn since starting to train as a Shadow. Something inside me is emerging from its cage, something that's been locked up for far too long. It's finally inching its way out of the dark and stepping in the light, becoming stronger and stronger every day as the light shines brighter and brighter.

While I'm snuggling into Everett's side, Dean finds a spot on the lounge beside us, settling in as he lets out a long sigh.

"Right, mates, we're here to discuss Sloan's progress on her training to provide a report to the higher-ups. They've been asking about her abilities and need an update," Everett addresses the room. He squeezes my shoulder slightly, reassuring me that I am on track in his eyes. To me, that's all that matters.

"Well, I can sure as shit say her combat skills are strong as hell. She keeps up the physical training, and she'll be able to take down a man three times her size." Dean looks over to me, giving me a slight head nod. Surely, he was referring to our moment in the shower. I give him a small smile, my cheeks getting warm.

"I second that—she almost slit my throat today." Arno's laugh fills the room, and I see Dean glance at Arno with eyebrows raised.

"Well, shit, why didn't you, baby girl?" Dean asks, cocking his head at me, genuinely wanting an answer as to why I didn't just go ahead and kill him. The banter between my guys is playful, but of course, I sometimes think they are actually serious

I shrug my shoulders as I look at Arno, giving him a small smile as he lifts his hands in a defensive position.

"Hey, she was the one who hesitated—she could've if she wanted to, mate. I guess I've started growing on her." Everett chuckles beside me before reeling us back in to continue the discussion.

As the three of them continue talking about me, I sit there, not fully listening, as they continue to boast about my training, along with areas that need improvement. Looking down at where my hands rest,

I see Colson's hair tie on my wrist. The seafoam-green braided band has sat there hugging my wrist since I found it on the floor of his bathroom.

I trace the braid with my fingers, remembering him wearing this very hair tie in his hair. His beautiful golden hair was expertly twisted into a bun, always letting loose a few strands that framed his face. My heart begins to ache as I close my eyes, remembering our short time together. The part of my heart that's healing begins to splinter once again whenever I think of him. His hazel eyes, his golden skin, the way he always put me front and center of his world. My golden retriever boy ripped away from me. He was stolen and brutalized before we could even live our lives.

The splinters in my heart become shards, stabbing the inside walls of my chest, causing me to bleed out. Pain quickly turns into rage from within. My blood boils hot with the image of Cara—her Hades-like smile forever imprinted in my mind. I will kill her, and I will smile while I do it.

When I open my eyes again, I see all three men staring at me, worry etched across their faces. They'd stopped talking, but I hadn't noticed. I was so caught up in the memories, the thoughts, the future, that I became lost in myself. My eyes drift to each of them before asking,

"What, what did I miss?" Arno clears his throat before scooting up in his chair and leaning his elbows on his knees.

"Listen to me, little one. I know you're angry, and rightfully so. We all are. But you need to listen to me when I say going into a scenario emotionally driven never ends well. Do you remember what I told you on the plane before we got to Shem's property?" I dig through my mind, trying to remember, but the only thing I can remember is holding Colson in my arms as the light slowly left his eyes. I shake my head, trying to get that image out of my head.

"I told you emotions get you killed. You need to learn to turn them off when it matters. Never turn them off completely, but you do need to learn to control them better."

I look at Dean, his expression rigid, and if I didn't know any better, I'd say he agrees with Arno. That would be a first. I then look to Everett, and he too, gives me a slight nod. His emerald eyes show a glimpse of understanding.

"There is a switch in the back of everyone's mind that controls the emotional portions of our brains. You need to learn how to turn it on and off when need be." I cock my head at Arno, not understanding his metaphor.

"How does one turn off an emotion?" I ask, genuinely curious as to how I am supposed to do that.

"You already know how, little one, you did it before you just don't remember. Right before I welcomed you to The Shadows when we were on the plane—do you remember? You looked up at me, closed your eyes, and when you opened them, you were Sloan reborn. That's the moment I knew you were going to become one of us. You tapped into that control. Now you need to do that again and home in on that skill." I nod before looking down at my hands again.

"How does one practice this?" I look back up at Arno, but he glances at Dean and then at Everett. I follow his line of sight, landing on Everett. "How?" I ask Everett, his eyes on me as he inhales deeply. He then rubs his hand down his face before standing up from where he sat beside me. He places his hands in his pant pockets and walks forward, lowering his head slightly, and stops—his back to me.

"Training is not hard physically. It's the emotional training that can break a person. It's tapping into the deepest, darkest traumas of one's life and bringing you to the forefront to experience it all over again. It's throwing you into a pit of vipers and expecting you not to react." Everett finally turns around, facing me before he continues. "It's the hardest part of becoming a Shadow—not many people pass this aspect of training." There is a long pause in the room as I absorb their words.

"I'll ask you this one last time, love. Are you one hundred percent certain this is what you want?" I look up at Everett, his face unreadable as he stares down at me. His large frame is stiff and unflinching. If I didn't know any better, I'd say he was holding his breath for my answer. I see the hair tie on my wrist one last time before looking back to Everett, my eyes hard and voice stern.

"I'm ready, this is who I'm meant to be." Out of the corner of my eye, I see Arno rubbing his hands together, his head nodding up and down. My eyes drift to Dean, his body slouched in the chair and arms lying perfectly on the armrests. His eyes are on mine, and I can't tell if he's happy, mad, sad—I don't know what he is feeling. I guess he's already mastered the art of turning his switch off.

Everett closes his eyes for a moment longer than expected. He hoped I would back out before this training phase began, but I'm all in, and nothing will stop me.

"Right, we start this phase of your training tomorrow." Everett then turns around and leaves the room before saying over his shoulder,

"I'll see you both at home. Get some rest, you'll need it, love. Have a good night, Arno." Then he exits the lounge and disappears down the hall without another word. What the hell have I gotten myself into?

CHAPTER 4

SLOAN

The ride home from headquarters is quiet. Sitting in the passenger seat, I start going through all the scenarios Everett could put me through that would assist me in controlling my emotions. This was Everett's specialty, controlling emotions in every situation you might find yourself in. I'd be lying if I said I wasn't nervous, but I knew this was just another step I needed to take to avenge Colson and finally take back my life.

Staring out the window, I'm lost in my thoughts, then a hand intertwines with mine, and I flinch at the sudden touch. Glancing over at Dean, I find he's still focused on the road ahead, but his firm hand in mine brings me back from the depths of my head.

"It's going to be hard—he's going to try to use your past trauma to break you from the inside out." He pauses, taking a deep breath before continuing, not once looking away from the road. "This was the hardest part of training for me. They beat me, shot me, drowned me—did everything imaginable that could break a man physically. Nothing compared to the emotional aspect. I'm not saying this to scare you, I'm saying this because if you go in there blind, not knowing how truly difficult it could get, there's no telling where your mind will take you."

"What do you mean no telling where my mind will take me?" I'm confused and not following what he's trying to get at. He squeezes my hand a little tighter.

"Sloan, you have a lot of traumas, more than most. What I don't want to happen is you leave your switch turned off and never turn it back on. You are strong, and I know you'll dominate this phase as you have with the other phases. What I'm worried about is losing who you are, losing the side of you we fell in love with. Emotions are dangerous, yes, but they're also mandatory in molding who we are as people. Before we got you, the three of us were living in a world where our switches were permanently in the off position. You flipped that switch for us, for me. If it weren't for you, we'd still be lost."

"Dean," is all I can say. I can feel the swell of tears lining the bottoms of my eyelids. Dean's words swim through my head as I try to comprehend what he's asking of me.

"I know you are capable of turning your switch off. I can't imagine you going through your childhood without having to turn it off sometimes. Please promise me, baby girl, you don't stay in that dark, emotionless pit that Everett is going to put you in. It may start to feel good not having to deal with your emotions, but I promise you, staying in that dimension will quickly become the loneliest place in the world."

I lower my eyes to where our hands intertwine. His long fingers wrap around my small delicate ones, his knuckles almost white from the pressure of his grasp. Holding tight as if I may disappear if he lets go. This man loves me, there is no questioning that, and I love him.

I think back to the day I was kidnapped; I was walking down the sidewalk towards my hostel after leaving the café. I wasn't being smart; I had no sense of my surroundings, and my earbuds were in my ears, I couldn't even hear if someone was approaching me. I was so naïve back then, a dumb young woman thinking she could take on this world all her own. Waking up that morning, I never imagined I would be bashed over the head and thrown into the back of a typical kidnapper van. Oh, how things have changed.

"I promise," I say in a whisper, reassuring Dean I wouldn't stay in the dark forever. I no longer want to be a victim, not now, not ever. Dean raises our hands to his mouth and kisses my fingers one by one. His warm lips linger on each one as my skin heats from his touch.

Arriving at the house, I make my way upstairs to get into more comfortable clothes, and by comfortable, I mean a pair of Colson's sweatpants and his t-shirt. I frequently gravitate to his room since losing him—we all do. The three of us have now permanently made Colson's bed ours. Everett, Dean, and I have slept in his bed for the past six months. It's the closest we can get to him without physically crawling into his grave.

Walking into his room, I head to his dresser and pull out my favorite pair of his gray sweatpants and white v-cut t-shirt. Stripping down my clothes, I bring them to the hamper in the bathroom, discarding them and begin stepping into the sweats.

Standing in the bathroom alone, I stare at my reflection in the mirror. "Hey, babe. How'd I do today with training?" I talk to him when I'm alone, as if he's still with me. "I got Arno good—I could've slit his throat even. You'd be proud of me." I pull my long blond hair back into a messy top bun, grabbing the seafoam hair tie from my wrist, and securing my hair with it.

Looking at my body as I start pulling his shirt over my head, I can see my muscles have become more prominent and fuller since starting six months ago. My arms are no longer stick thin, and my legs have become more defined. Glancing away from the mirror, I catch a glimpse of Dean leaning against the door frame. His arms resting against the top of the frame as his long torso leans forward. His eyes are on me as he gives me a small smile.

Dean has also changed into a pair of sweats, but he has chosen to go shirtless—my favorite outfit. I walk over to him, wrap my arms around his waist, and squeeze him tight. Long arms drape over my shoulders as he rests his head on me, hugging me back.

"Damn, baby girl, I miss the fuck out of him." His voice is a mere whisper as he breathes into my hair, his voice laced with sadness.

"I do too." My voice shakes as I respond, his hold on me tightening. We stay in each other's arms for a moment, the feeling of pain and loss filling the room around us.

The sound of a phone chiming breaks me from Dean's hold as he reaches into his pocket to grab his cell.

"Sorry, love, its headquarters. I need to take this." Dean kisses the top of my forehead and leaves the room as he answers the call. I watch his back as he leaves the room and turns to head down the hallway. Standing in the doorway to the bathroom, I let my eyes wander around Colson's room. My eyes roam from his dresser to his wall posters to his nightstand. Everything remains untouched, unchanged, except for his bed, of course. We've left his room exactly how it was the last time he was here. My chest tightens and aches as I make my way over to his bed and sit beside his nightstand.

A lone picture frame sits atop his nightstand, and I lean over to pick it up. I've seen this picture before. Colson is standing in the middle between Dean and Everett after what looks to be a training day when they were younger. Colson's hair was shorter then. I rub my fingers along his face, a smile stretching across his plump lips as the three of them embrace in the typical bro hug, arms draped over one another. I smile down at him, a single tear falling from my cheek and landing on the glass.

I lift the photo to my lips and kiss his face, a small sob escaping me before I return the frame to the nightstand. I quickly wipe the wetness from my face, internally scolding myself for crying again. Just as I collect myself, I go to stand up from the bed, but something peeking out from his nightstand catches my eye. I pull the drawer open, and I'm met with a small brown notebook. The edges are worn, and it looks like someone tried to destroy it at one point but decided against it.

Picking up the small book, I hold it in my fingers, turning it over but finding no writing on the outside. Opening the cover, I see the word *journal* in small print on the first page. Is this Colson's private journal? I hadn't known he kept a journal. I hesitate a moment, wondering if I should be reading his personal thoughts. I can't—this is an invasion of privacy even though he's gone.

I go to put the journal back in the nightstand, but a quick gust of cool air has my hair on the back of my neck standing straight up. I sit up straighter, looking around and noticing the windows are all shut, and the central air hasn't kicked on yet.

I take a deep breath before whispering to myself, "Colson, is that you?" Suddenly, the picture frame falls face down on the nightstand, making me gasp at the sudden noise. I've never believed in the paranormal or the supernatural, but what happens next is unexplainable.

"Do you want me to read your journal, babe?" I scan the room awaiting his response, and when his bathroom door slams shut, I instantly stand from where I'm sitting, a small scream escaping me. He's here. Colson's with me right now as I clutch his journal in my hands. A light sheen of sweat layers my skin, and my throat instantly becomes dry as I nod my head.

"Okay, I'll read it," I breathe out before sitting back down on his bed and opening Colson's journal to the first page.

CHAPTER 5

SLOAN

October 21, 2021

I've been told I need to start writing in this journal by Janice, The Shadows' therapist. She thinks this will help clear my mind. I've been tasked with a rising number of child abduction cases, and she thinks this is slowly getting to me. I can't say it's not, but I don't necessarily think writing in this journal will help anything. Whatever to keep the organization happy, I guess. Plus, they said if I don't cooperate with the therapist, I'll be suspended from further missions until she deems me mentally fit enough to continue. Let me put this on paper and say I think this is bullshit. I guess this is entry one. Fuck.

After reading Colson's first entry, I slam the journal close, grasping it to my chest as the sting of tears builds behind my eyes. I take a few deep breaths, calming myself and focusing on not allowing more tears to fall.

"Are you alright, doll?" Dean's voice fills the room. Standing from the bed, I make my way over to Dean, stretching out my arm and handing him the small journal. Dean then glances at the journal, then back up at me before taking it from my fingers and flipping through the pages one by one. It takes him a moment to respond. Before he looks up from the pages, his eyes begin turning a shade of red.

"Is this Colson's journal? Where did you find it?" I don't speak, I point to the nightstand. His eyes dart to the nightstand, then back to me. "I don't understand," he says to me, confusion etched across his face.

"What do you mean?" What could he possibly be confused about? This is Colson's journal; from the sounds of it, no one knew he was keeping a diary.

"When we see the organization's therapist, she tells us to keep journals for our thoughts." I stare at Dean, furrowing my eyebrows, trying to understand his confusion.

"When we start keeping journals, we have to keep them at headquarters. Under no circumstance are we allowed to take the journals home with us. If this were to end up in the wrong hands, it could reveal top secret information exposing our whole operation."

I look back down at the journal; every page has been written on. More than one hundred entries, all kept hidden in his nightstand. What secrets had he kept within those pages? Why had he taken it home if it were deemed dangerous to take from the confines of headquarters? The tension in the room was becoming thick, both mine and Dean's minds racing with theories as to why Colson brought this home, putting both Dean and Everett in possible danger.

Just then, the sound of the front door slamming echoes throughout the foyer.

"We should show this to Everett." His voice is above a whisper, and I nod my head in agreement. We both make our way downstairs, heading towards the kitchen, where I hear the fridge open and close. Walking into the kitchen, I see Everett leaning his back against the counter, taking a long sip from his freshly opened beer. His face appears flustered as he brushes his hair back from his face.

Out of his peripherals, he sees Dean and I step through the arched doorway, Dean holding the journal close to his side. As I come into view from behind Dean, Everett's eyes are on me. A small smile pulling at the corner of his mouth, the stress he was holding visibly easing from between his eyebrows. Setting his beer on the island, he steps towards me, hooks his hands underneath my arms, and hoists me onto the island, where he nestles into me between my legs. Wrapping my arms around his neck, I hold him close to my breasts, his muscular frame melting into mine as the tension of a long day slowly evaporates off him.

"I need you tonight, baby girl. I need you so

fucking bad." His voice is muffled as he presses his face into my body, tightening his hold. There is something off about his voice. He's holding something back, an emotion he doesn't want to show. Although Everett is the master at controlling emotions, he always appears to be fighting an internal battle with allowing any of his feelings to show. As Dean said earlier, there is a switch within us, and we control when and if we turn it off. At this moment, Everett's emotional switch is turned off, but it's apparent he's struggling with allowing it to turn back on. What is he hiding from?

"Listen, mate, we need to show you something," Dean chimes in, causing Everett to rise from beneath the comfort of my arms. Straightening his posture, he turns around facing Dean, but still leans back between my legs and rests his arms on the top of my thighs. Draping my arms around his chest, I let Dean take the lead with this, since the two of them know the policies of the organization. Letting out a deep sigh, Dean lifts the journal and hands it to Everett.

"It looks like Colson had been keeping a journal assigned to him by the therapist," Dean says nothing more, allowing Everett to connect the dots. Taking the journal, he looks up at Dean.

"Where did you find this?"

"I found it in his nightstand a moment ago," I answer before Dean. Everett then begins flipping through the journal, stopping to skim the contents of the small book before finally closing it and tossing it to the island. The journal makes a loud slap as it lands on the granite countertop, making me flinch at the sudden noise.

"He knew the policy. Why would he risk it, risk all our safety by bringing it here?" It's the question we're all thinking.

"Have you read it?" Everett glances over his shoulder, awaiting my answer.

"Only the first entry. He wrote how he was told by the therapist to keep a journal, but that was it. I haven't read any further," I answer as Everett lifts himself from where he leans against me and makes his way to the cabinet that holds his favorite bourbon. Proceeding to pour himself a glass, he lifts the decanter to Dean and me, but the both of us shake our heads, refusing his offer for a drink.

The three of us remain in silence as Everett looks to be pondering his thoughts by the way his forehead creases with every sip he takes. Crossing my legs in front of me, I clasp my hands together and start to fiddle with my fingers. I stare over at Dean, his face lowered to the ground and his muscular arms crossed in front of his chest, looking equally as pensive as Everett.

"Who wants to work out?" I hop off the counter and give them both a sympathetic smile in hopes they will allow their minds to rest and take my bait. As the two of them look at me, I can see the tension releasing from their shoulders as they each give me a crooked smile.

"Just what I need, baby girl," Everett responds as he sets his glass down and walks over to me, hoisting me over his shoulder. "Dean, you coming?" With a sharp slap to my ass, Everett makes his way to the hallway leading to the gym, Dean following close behind us. Pushing my hands against Everett's back, I purse my lips at Dean. There's no hesitation—he leans in and kisses me with his full lips as the three of us make our way to the gym.

"You better be saving some for me, princess." Everett lets out a chuckle from behind us as he squeezes my ass in his hand.

"Plenty to go around, boss man." I lean down his back and give his ass a playful squeeze back.

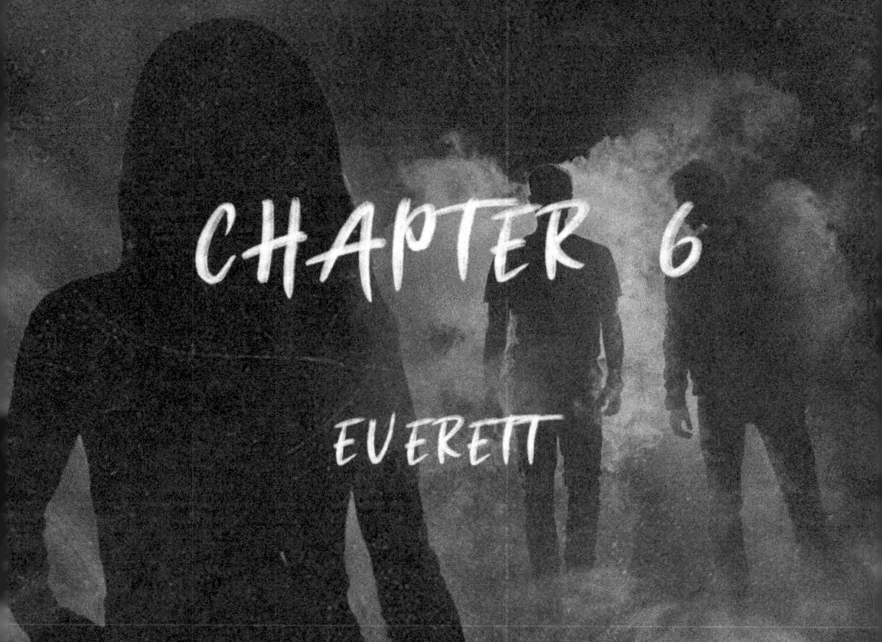

CHAPTER 6

EVERETT

October 24, 2021

I have no idea how to start these fucking entries, but whatever. I was tasked with a target two days ago that got me thinking quite a bit. The target is a forty-seven-year-old male who's made a reputation in the skin trade business. Reading his file, it lists his very active involvement in the dark web that specializes in the buying and selling of underage girls. This shit makes my blood boil. His file also states that he himself is a father to three preteen girls himself. That's the shit I don't understand. A father himself, buying and selling young girls to predators that will do unthinkable shit to them. I'm glad to take this man's life. I wish I could do it in a more brutal way other than a quick blast to the head with a bullet. He deserves a more painful and slow death.

• • •

The three of us work out for the remainder of the evening. Dean and I focus on Sloan's takedown ability and grappling skills on the mat. After they found Colson's journal, my mind instantly began racing with unanswered questions. Questions that will never be answered due to the fact that the only one who could answer them is no longer here. Fuck, I miss him so damn much.

While on the mats with Sloan, I can't help but admire her new confidence and strength. She has put her all into training, and the once delicate and fragile woman has bloomed into a fighting machine. Her ability to absorb every aspect of The Shadows' training is on a higher level than most. Not only has she been successful in taking down an opponent twice her size, she's also mastered the skill of reading her opponents every move before they've executed it. Dean has been working with her nonstop in this area of training, and it shows. The growth over the past six months has been a roller coaster of emotions for me personally. Although I'm more than proud she is learning to defend herself in any scenario, I'm also concerned about her future. I know for the three of us, The Shadows' lifestyle is brutal and much more mentally debilitating than physically.

Watching her take down Dean on the mat, my amusement fades as I think of the emotional stress that she'll soon have to endure in her training. Sloan's physical capabilities are of no concern for me. That's apparent with the way she slams Dean flat on his back after successfully escaping his grasps. However, her mind is no longer going to be safe come tomorrow.

Strength is not always something you can see. It comes in forms that we, as humans, cannot see with the naked eye. The mind is a dangerous yet powerful place that houses a muscle that is the hardest to strengthen. Whereas a bicep or quad can be stretched and torn to rebuild itself stronger and more durable, the mind is a whole new world—a whole new area of the body that needs to be treated with far more care than most. We have to protect ourselves, guard our minds, or we can crumble far too quickly.

The sweet sound of her laughter brings me back to the mats. Glancing over, I see Sloan straddling Dean with a smile that screams victorious, and I can't help myself, I smile at the two of them. Their playfulness is intoxicating and infectious, and some days, I wish I could see the joys from her perspective. I fear I've lost my ability to be 'fun' and for that, I pray she never loses hers.

After a few more rounds of the two of them sparring, we decide to sit in the sauna. The steam and heat releasing the tightness in our muscles as we melt into the wooden benches we've all sprawled out on. Sloan has taken the top bench lying flat on her back, her legs crossed in front of her as her arms lie by her sides. Dean is sitting closest to the door; he never has the strength to last in the sauna for long periods of time. Pussy. I've taken the bench below Sloan, my back facing her as I spread my legs wide and drape my arms over the top bench where Sloan is lying.

"When are your birthdays?" A chuckle slips from Dean's mouth as I tilt my head back to Sloan. "I'm serious! When were you guys born?" Looking into her crystal-blue eyes, I give her a small smile before Dean answers first.

"January first." I can see her smile from my peripherals, allowing her a moment before I answer her question as well.

"December twenty-third."

"Ooo almost a Christmas baby," Sloan says, not looking at either of us.

"Do you guys want to know mine?" she asks, not knowing we already know her birthday, what hospital she was born at, how long her mother labored for, and the weather on that day. I play along, though.

"What's your birthday, love?"

"September sixteenth," she says, drawing out the words. "I've never celebrated my birthday before, not once. To me, it's merely another day if I'm being honest." I understand that. Dean, Colson, and I have never celebrated our birthdays; we were never celebrated as kids nor as recruits in training, so why start now? There was a long pause before she spoke again.

"When was Colson's birthday?" I knew that question was coming, and I dreaded having to tell her. Glancing over to Dean, I see he's already staring at me, his eyes hard as he inhales a deep breath. I close my eyes and rest the back of my head on the bench once more.

"September sixteenth," I breathe out. I keep my eyes closed as Dean and I wait for her to react. I hear movement from behind me as she rolls her body from her back to her front.

"Oh," is all she says. Nothing more. I sit up, lifting my head and turning to look at her. Damn, she's beautiful—her completely naked body glistening with sweat across her skin, pooling at the curve of her ass where her two dimples are. Turning sideways, I lightly place my fingers at the base of her neck and traced the line of sweat down to the top of her ass. She crosses her arms and lays her head down on top of them, closing her eyes and enjoying the sensation. Goosebumps rise on her skin as I do this, over and over again, with my fingers.

"What's going on in your head, doll?" Dean's deep husky voice asks her from across the sauna. She opens her eyes to this question, staring at him from where her head is resting.

"Arno told me something the other day." I pinch my brows together, the sound of his name on her lips sparking a feeling inside me I'm unfamiliar with. The two of them have grown close over the past six months. Not only training together but also the rescue attempts they both carried out to get Dean, Colson, and myself out of Ireland. He was there for her when we couldn't be. I was thankful for him, but I'd be lying if I said I wasn't jealous of their new friendship. All I have to say is, that's all it better be—a friendship and nothing more. The devil help him if he ever tried to do anything more.

"He told me birthdays are simply a celebration of an event that occurred, a date that someone deems special. He said you could make any date an event to be celebrated, such as birth, a wedding, or death. I didn't understand at the time when he said celebrating someone's death. Why would anyone want to celebrate a death?" Dean and I stare at one another, confused at what she's trying to tell us. But then she continues, "I understand now what he was saying. I'm going to celebrate every year on the day I kill Cara. For Colson."

I turn and look at her. She's unflinching as she remains with her head down. The tension returns to her shoulders, and she speaks again. "I'm going to celebrate her death every fucking year as if it were Christmas or New Year's. I'm going to celebrate the day I eliminate her from this earth for taking Colson from us." She then stands from the bench and leaves the two of us in the sauna. Anger radiates from her perfect body as she walks between us, slamming the door behind her.

"She's holding too much anger, mate. She's going to get herself hurt if she doesn't learn to control that better." Dean is right; she needs to filter her anger more efficiently. Anger is one of the more dangerous emotions.

"She'll learn soon enough, mate," I retort, standing and exiting the sauna, Dean following close behind.

CHAPTER 7

SLOAN

October 28th, 2021

Killing my last target had me thinking twice about my humanity. Usually, we are given a target along with a place and time to carry out the job. This particular job had me eliminating the target at a fucking family dinner! His three daughters had to witness his brains being splattered all over their spaghetti dinner. Fuck, seriously? I felt nothing as I pulled the trigger until I saw the expression on the youngest daughter's face. Another image that will forever be burned in the back of my mind. Oh well, she's better off without that slimy bastard, if I'm being completely honest.

Everett's taken Colson's journal, informing us that he would read through the contents to see if there are any clues as to why he brought the journal home with him. After I leave the sauna, I head upstairs to take a shower, my anger reaching a new level after learning that Colson and I share the same birth date. Cara stole him from me, stole a future, and I intend to end her life in the most brutal of ways.

Standing underneath the spray of the water, I let my hair fall over my face. Trying to calm myself down. I begin taking long, deep breaths and counting to ten—a trick Arno started making me do when he saw I couldn't control my anger very well. I've never felt anger like this before. It's new to me, and fuck, is it hard to manage. I feel it in my blood, a raging fire that spreads so rapidly I can't distinguish it. Everett assured me his training will open my eyes to emotional control, and to be honest, I'm ready for it. I need to get a better hold on myself, I fear some days the anger will never leave, and I will forever be burning from the inside out.

After about eight deep breaths, I can feel my muscles relaxing and my jaw unclenching. Lifting my head to the water I let it rain down on my face, hoping it will wash away everything—every emotion, every feeling, all the bitter thoughts swirling in my head. I want to be numb; I don't want to feel anything at all for the rest of the night. I want to feel like me. Whatever "me" feels like. Who was I before all this happened to me?

I slap my hands against the tile wall, making a loud splat that echoes against the walls.

"Fuck!" I whisper-yell, the hold on my emotions

quickly slipping as more intrusive thoughts rapidly form in my head.

"Think of your happiest memory." Everett's voice startles me, and I jump back, looking at him through the shower's glass door. "Hold on to the memory when your emotions start consuming you. Hold on to it and allow your mind to fill with only that one thought. This will redirect your mind away from the emotional chaos you're feeling and focus solely on that one memory." He opens the glass door, steam billowing out around him as he leans his forearm against the glass.

"Think of a memory, Sloan. Go on, tell me when you have it." I do as he says, closing my eyes and trying to think of a moment when I'm truly happy and nothing else matters. Thoughts of my father immediately fill my head, his firm hand, his cigars, and his constant yelling. I then turn my mind to my mother, the blank stare always occupying her beautiful blue eyes, her body always slouched over from being entirely drugged out.

"Sloan, stop. Look at me." His voice is firm, and when I open my eyes he's right there, standing right in front of me. He's fully clothed and quickly becoming soaked from the spray of the water. Placing his palm against my cheek he says again, "The happiest memory you have, even if it's merely a dream or a vision you imagined in your head. Don't allow anyone else in your head, this is your space." I try again, closing my eyes and focusing on anything that brings me even the slightest bit of joy in my life. When I think it's no use, I see him. Colson. Sitting at the edge of the pool with his legs dangling in the water. He's smiling, his long blond hair tousled as it blows in the wind around him. His golden skin gleaming as the sun shines down on him, the hazel and gold flecks of color reflecting the sun's rays. There he is, sitting there staring at me, and nothing else matters.

"Now, love, hold on to that memory. Whenever your anger begins to overflow, or your rage, sadness, confusion, or any other feeling becomes uncontrollable, think of that and only that." I stay like this for a long moment, the warm water spraying down on me, my eyes closed, and Colson appears behind my eyelids. Calming my storm from within.

When I open my eyes, Everett is still there, but so is Dean. Leaning against the vanity, they both watch as I finally feel relaxed in my skin. Letting out a long sigh, I look at Everett.

"Thank you." He truly is the master of emotional control. I haven't felt this calm in a long while. For so long, I've felt as though I've been living in a straitjacket of emotions that've slowly begun to cripple me and my sanity. I push my wet hair back from my face and turn off the shower. Everett hands me my towel and I take it, wrapping it tight around my body. Stepping out of the shower, I pull all my hair to the side squeezing it to remove the excess water.

"Is that how your emotional training will go?" I

ask Everett, as I continue to get the water out of my hair. I don't miss the look he gives Dean before he answers me.

"Nothing I do here will prepare you for that. Whatever memory you chose, I hope it's a strong one, baby girl."

The next day, the three of us drive to headquarters without a single word spoken between us. The radio plays "This is War" by Thirty Seconds to Mars as we pull into the parking lot. If I wasn't nervous before, I sure as shit am now. I am good at physical training, the beatings, bruises, and muscle aches, but there is something daunting about rummaging through someone's mental trauma.

Everett pulls into his usual parking spot and turns off the G-Class before letting out a sigh and turning to face me. I remain still, his hot gaze on the side of my face burning a hole straight into my brain.

"Listen, everything that happens today and the coming week, I need you to know this is all training. Nothing is real—your mind is going to trick you—but you need to do as I said and focus on the one memory. Hold on to it and don't let it go. No matter how long each scenario plays out." Everett's voice is full of pain, and it sounds like he's just as nervous as I am, maybe even more so. I nod slowly, remembering my memory of Colson and replaying it over and over in my mind.

"How long is today going to be?" I ask, not entirely sure why because every other training day was just that, a full day. I'm not sure why I expect anything different. It isn't until I turn my head to Everett that I notice he's looking at Dean in the rearview mirror, concern etched across his face.

I'm about to turn around to Dean, a sharp prick crashes into the side of my shoulder, causing me to scream out. As I grab the place on my shoulder, a burning sensation begins creeping down my arm and up my neck. Opening my mouth, I realize I can't speak, I can't move—I'm paralyzed in the passenger seat. My vision quickly fades to black, the familiar ring of darkness consuming my eyes. The last thing I remember is someone saying, "We love you, baby girl. Remember to hold on." My eyes close, and the sensation of being weightless and utterly alone has me slipping into the darkness.

CHAPTER 8

SLOAN

September 2, 2021

I don't feel like this journal shit is doing anything for me. I don't see how my writing in this thing will somehow magically fix all the broken pieces of my insides. We're all broken and will forever be broken—that's the nature of the business. Plus, I think if we allow ourselves to be soft and one with our emotions all the time, it will ultimately get us killed. I get not wanting to become a zombie to our work, but fuck, when you kill people for a living, what the hell do you expect? You can't get connected to people, you can't put yourself in their shoes, or fall in love for that matter. This puts them at risk, as well as myself. So, yeah, I guess I am a fucking zombie. It's not the life I chose willingly. I was created, so was every one of us. We were thrown into this life, and now we're expected to still have a conscience. Not happening, mate.

. . .

My head feels like a sledgehammer has been thumping against my skull, the sharp ache making it hard to open my eyes. Forcing myself to peel my eyelids open, I have to blink several times before my hazy vision starts too slowly clear. When I finally manage to regain my eyesight, my breath hitches in my throat, and I can't believe where I am.

Sitting straight up from the dirty carpet, the scent of cigarette smoke and alcohol invades my nose, causing me to choke. Coughing as I try to stand on shaking legs, I spin around, gaping at the sight before me. I'm in my room in my parent's house. How the fuck did I get here? Was I sent back to the States? My chest tightens, and I feel as though I can't catch my breath. I can feel my throat constricting, and I begin hyperventilating, panic grabbing my insides and squeezing the life out of me.

My bed, my dresser, the yellowish walls from smoke, my cracked window, and the fire escape stairs leading to the roof where I used to hide from this place. Everything is exactly how I left it the day I ran away on my eighteenth birthday. This can't be happening; this can't be real. How? Why?

I rub my head, trying to remember how I got here, when I got here, anything. But I can't. I don't have a single thought in my head except for fear. The same fear that consumed me my entire life while living within these walls. My eyes begin to sting, the fear becoming all too much, and then I hear him. My father.

"Sloan!" his voice bellows down the hallway. "Sloan, don't you hide from me, you little bitch!" My blood runs cold as I begin backing up towards my window. *No, no, no, this isn't real Sloan, this can't be real.* My door flies open, my father standing at the threshold clutching a beer can while the other hand holds tight to a cigarette. I quit—literally stop— breathing. This man who caused so much pain, so much trauma, so much hate, is standing in front of me as a wicked smile stretches across his sweat-covered face.

"Ahh, there you are. Have you missed me?" His words are like venom burning across my skin—his plaque-covered teeth, or lack thereof, showing through cracked lips. He looks awful, the drugs and alcohol tinting his skin in a reddish hue, inflammation consuming his whole body. Pockmarks cover his cheeks and forehead, evidence of the harder drugs he's now taken a liking to. No shock there.

"You were late coming home from school today— that's not good. My friends were expecting a play- date with you, and now I won't be getting paid. That means someone is getting punished. That person is you." Then, he rushes towards me, dropping his cigarette and beer can as he barrels into me, my body slamming against the window, causing it to splinter more. I yell out as I try to grab his hands that are gripped around my neck. His hold is tight as he squeezes harder, constricting my windpipe. I can't breathe. He's so heavy, so angry, as his beady eyes are on mine. Redness filling the once white in his eyes.

Thrashing and kicking against him, he doesn't budge, not even a little. Black circles start to form around the outskirts of my vision. My breathing is completely gone—no air in, no air out. The blackness grows more and more until there's nothing left. My eyes close. This is it; this is how I go. I didn't see that coming.

The pressure that was once around my neck suddenly disappears, and I suck in a greedy amount of air as I choke to fill my lungs. Coughing hard, I open my eyes, expecting to see the ceiling of my bedroom, but I don't. Harsh overhead lights blind me as I try to focus and regain my breath. Someone's shaking my shoulders. Large hands grip me tightly as I hear my name being called out.

"Sloan. Sloan, wake up, you can breathe. Take it easy, try to slow down and breathe normally. You need to hold on, you forgot to hold on, my love." Everett, was that Everett's voice? Squinting hard, I see his silhouette against the lights, a perfect outline of his gorgeous face staring down at me.

"Whe-where am I? What the fuck was that?" I cough out, gripping my chest as the sensation of being choked slowly releases its grasp on me. I hear a deep sigh before I'm lifted to a sitting position, a firm body sitting behind me, propping me up with their own.

"That was your first lesson in emotional training.

It's our virtual reality simulation of your worst fears, traumas, and memories you've buried deep down. It brings to light these moments for you to relive them. Feel the same pain in hopes that you react in a different way," Everett replies, his tone laced with something, but I can't pinpoint it, especially not at this moment.

"I-I—it felt so real," I choke out, holding in the tears that threaten to slip. It felt so fucking real. I'm not scared though, I feel angry. I feel enraged, and all I want to do is punch something. I stand abruptly, steadying myself before turning on Everett and now Dean, who's getting up off the floor behind me.

"Why wouldn't you warn me? Why throw me into something like that? You both know how bad it was! You knew!" I'm so angry I can't stop the words from coming. I'm angry and want them to know. "You could have given me a little heads up before I was almost choked to death!" I'm yelling and my posture goes rigid as I spit my words. The look on their faces are expressions I've never seen from them. They look scared, they look guilty, as their eyes soften on me. They both stand there, their eyes pleading and apologetic.

"How could you do—"

"Little one, we know you're mad, but you want to be a Shadow? This is what it takes to be one of us. You think Everett and Dean wanted to see you go through that? You need to toughen the fuck up. That was level one, wait until the more difficult levels. I suggest you take a walk, cool down, and remember why you're here training in the first place." Arno's deep voice comes from behind me as he walks into the virtual reality room with the three of us. Turning on him, I give him a deep scowl, my anger uncontrollable at this point.

"Get your little ass to the gym. I'll be there in a minute, and we can spar so you can get that rage out." I say nothing. I walk past him, not giving the guys another look. Reaching the door, I tear it open and begin to step through, but I hear them speak and I freeze.

"Her anger is getting worse. She's locked up her rage for too long, and now it's coming out, and she can't control it. Like mine was." Dean's voice is a punch to the gut. The door closes behind me, and I lean my back against it, releasing a deep breath. I didn't want to snap at them—they were doing exactly what I asked for. I asked for all of this. Everett, Dean, Arno, and Colson all went through this same training. Each one experiencing their traumas in hopes of learning how to control their emotions. I shouldn't have yelled at them. Guilt quickly takes hold of me as the anger begins to dissipate within me.

I enter the gym with my head down. I feel like shit remembering the expressions Everett and Dean both gave me as I screamed in their faces. What's wrong with me? I should've known that was a test. Making my way over to the punching bag, I begin a one-two combo, starting off slowly and getting into a rhythm.

Once I'm warm enough, I pick up my speed, throwing in uppercuts and jabs as I practice my footwork.

Increasing my speed even more, I spin around, throwing out my arm, expecting to feel the give of the punching bag, but a strong hand grabs my forearm and swings me around as I land on my back. A knee presses hard into my chest, rendering me immobile.

"I expect better from you, little one. Next time you feel the need to act like a scared little pussy again, remember why you're here. Or did you forget already?" Arno's face is mere inches from mine as he speaks down to me. "Did you think this was going to be easy? Did you think it was going to be a walk in the fucking park? How do you think we became this way? You're no coffee-bitch anymore. You're training to be a fucking mercenary, so act like one."

He releases the hold he has on me, and I suck in a deep breath, pain stretching across my sternum from his knee. He stands, offering me his hand. Grabbing his hand, he lifts me to my feet, patting my back hard with his large hand.

"Don't expect at any point for this to be easy, little one." I nod my understanding, looking down at the mat, thoroughly embarrassed by my behavior. I try to swallow the lump in my throat, but I can't. Arno lifts my chin with his long fingers until I'm looking up at him. A tear slides down my cheek. I close my eyes, trying not to let any more escape. A finger brushes the tear from my cheek, and I open my eyes to Arno. The corner of his mouth turns up, giving me a sympathetic smile.

"That must have been hard. This shit sucks, I know." With that, I break down, the tears now a steady stream down my face as the images of my irate father play across my vision. Arno pulls me into his body, wrapping his muscular arms around me and holding me tight. I wrap my arms around his waist and rest my head against his chest, allowing my tears to fall freely. He's warm, and his hold on me is comforting as we stand there together. He lets me cry, he lets me feel, he lets me empty myself of the pain I've held onto for so long. Arno is with me, as he's been since we started this journey together, and I'm thankful he's here.

CHAPTER 9

DEAN

September 6, 2021

What the hell are we doing as an organization? We're trained to kill, eliminate, and be invisible. Why are the three of us now being tasked to kidnap some poor girl off the street? Everett, Dean, and I have rarely ever been tasked with the same mission, but today we received news that we would be doing a 'retrieve the target and deliver said target' job together and then dropping her off at an unknown location. What the fuck is this nonsense? We've had snatch-and-grab jobs before, but this one is cryptic with such minimal information, that it has me confused as hell. I think I speak for both Everett and Dean when I say this feels wrong and completely out of our job requirements. Fuck, we'll see how this goes, I guess.

. . .

The look on her face was soul-shattering. Her eyes were swelling with tears as she yelled at both Everett and me for not giving her a proper heads-up. I understand where she's coming from and why she's upset, but our hands were tied. We gave her more of a warning than any other recruit would have received. Nevertheless, my chest is tight with guilt, and I can hardly stand the idea of her being angry with me.

Walking down the hallway towards the gym, I want to help her get her anger out and offer myself up as her punching bag. I need to make amends with her immediately, and if that means I let her beat the shit out of me, so be it. Turning the corner, I head towards the gym doors that look to be propped open. As I make my way down, I hear the faint sounds of a sob. Is she crying?

Picking up my pace, I'm instantly halted at the doorway when my eyes land on her. She's wrapped in his arms—Arno's. She's clutching him desperately as tears stream down her face and soft cries slip from her mouth. My chest bubbles with guilt, but it's not until Arno threads his fingers through her hair and holds her head to his chest that my guilt instantly flips to rage. My entire body tense as he starts massaging her scalp as she continues to cry into his chest.

This is too intimate, too sensual for a comforting gesture. He shouldn't even be the one to comfort her. It should be me or Everett—no one else touches her.

Not like this.

I want to walk in there, grab him by the throat, and squeeze until he can't inhale another breath. My skin is vibrating with anger, and just as I'm about to take a step towards them, a firm hand lands on my shoulder.

"Don't, mate. Let her cry it out. He's not a threat," Everett whispers behind me. How can he say that? Is he not seeing what I'm seeing?

Without turning around to face him, I respond, "Sure appears more than a comforting embrace, mate." I growl as my eyes remain locked on them. Everett's hand releases me as he steps up beside me, the both of us looking on at our girl in the arms of another man. "He should know not to touch what isn't his." My skin is on fire, jealousy coursing through every inch, every pore of my being.

"If you go in there like that, what are you teaching her about emotional control?" Everett says as he stands in front of me, blocking my line of sight. He's right. What would I be teaching her? That I, myself, am a hothead and react before thinking. Fuck.

"Thank you, Arno. Will you give us a moment with our girl, please?" Everett says out loud, not turning away from me as he gives me a stern look. Glancing over his shoulder, I see Sloan pulling away from Arno's embrace, quickly wiping away her tears before either of us can notice. She shouldn't be embarrassed to cry in front of us. Why is she so comfortable with Arno? Something in my gut doesn't feel right about this friendship. Call me jealous, call me whatever you want, but my gut is rarely wrong.

Arno nods his head once to Everett, but turns back to Sloan once more.

"Are you okay, little one?" he asks her, and she immediately nods her head and gives him a small smile. My chest is heaving now, anger boiling in my chest. Arno turns on his heels and makes his way towards the both of us, still standing in the doorway. He tilts his head to Everett, and as he walks past him, he slaps a hand on my shoulder, giving it a small squeeze before heading down the hallway behind me.

I turn my head and glance at Arno as I watch his frame disappear around the corner at the end of the hall. I debate following him and telling him exactly how I feel about his little therapy session with my girl, but decide against it. I hear Everett and Sloan talking quietly behind me. Turning to join them, I see Sloan has wrapped her arms around Everett's waist, resting her head on his chest as she speaks.

"I'm so sorry, Everett, I shouldn't have reacted that way. You're just doing what I asked. This is a part of training, and I should've known this part would be hard. You warned me, and I didn't listen. I'm so sorry," she pleads into his chest, his hand resting on her head as the other wraps around her back, holding her tight.

"Don't apologize. This is always the most difficult part for everyone. It's not easy reliving the past, especially one so traumatic." Everett's tone is soft and comforting. I can see her shoulders relax into him as the tension slowly eases from her small frame. I stand there a moment longer, watching her and him, their bodies fusing together as one. Watching her now, I can't remember why I was mad a moment ago. Her love and loyalty to him is evident, an embrace entirely different from the one she shared with Arno. She melts into Everett's arms, allowing his words to fill her until her tears no longer fall down her beautiful face. I go from guilt to jealousy to anger and back to guilt in a fraction of a second as my eyes remain trained on her.

In this moment, I realize that no matter how much we train our emotions, we will forever battle the silent war within ourselves to keep them at bay. Our feelings come and go depending on the scenarios we are placed in. We fight against our anger, rage, jealousy, guilt, sadness, and so much more. This fight is a daily occurrence—a daily battle—that we will forever find ourselves in. This is why emotional training is so prevalent in The Shadows' training; this is the one constant of our lives that we will never master. Rather, we continue to work on it for the rest of our existence. She will forever battle her own war within, and it's up to us to support and be here for her, especially when she seems to be on the losing side of the war. Both of us will be here.

Always and forever.

CHAPTER 10

SLOAN

September 12, 2021

The three of us have decided on the date. The snatch-and-grab job will take place in four days' time. We've been given a date on which the package needs to be delivered, thus giving us four days to prep. We have yet to be given the location of the drop, which is confusing to say the least. Typically, by this point, we are given every detail needed to be successful. Everett told both Dean and I that he thinks something is of. Something doesn't feel right about this one, and I can't agree with him more. Preparation is key with this one, and we just don't know; and not knowing is dangerous.

After pouring my heart out to Everett and Dean, I couldn't stop apologizing for how I acted after my first training with the virtual reality simulation. I was a bitch and had no right to treat them that way. Arno quickly brought me back to reality. His sternness with me was exactly what I needed. I'm used to being coddled by my guys, that sometimes I turn into this prissy, self-righteous princess that needs a good kick in the ass. Enter the room, Arno. I'm thankful for his firm hand with me—this is something Everett and Dean will never do. Their love for me overpowers all else—which is not a bad thing, and in no way am I complaining—it's just they will never be the disciplinary teachers that I need sometimes. This role falls upon Arno, and I'm not sure he is mad about it either. He is the perfect big brother figure—hard, but gentle.

I woke up early this morning, my nerves getting the best of me for what training is to come today. Day two of emotional training and my mind is racing with what past event is going to be the key focus today. It's four thirty in the morning, and I'm on my second cup of coffee already. Sitting at the island alone, I sip my coffee, staring into my mug as I relive my childhood in my head over and over again.

Will it be the time my father used my body as his personal ashtray? Will it be one of the times my father's friends came to my room for their turn with me? Maybe it will be the time I ran away from home, just to be brought back by the cops. My father beat me so badly, that I passed out after the cops left. I didn't realize I had started crying until a tear lands in my mug, causing the liquid to splash and form ripples.

Fuck, stop crying, Sloan. You're not there anymore, you're free, no point in crying anymore.

Wiping my face clean, I take my coffee to the sliding glass door overlooking the pool outside. I peer to the crystal-blue water—the light illuminating the liquid from below, creating an ominous glow over the backyard. My eyes land on the edge of the pool where Colson and I had sex for the first time. I smile and close my eyes, remembering how he looked, how he felt against my skin—his touch on me. Goosebumps begin pricking my skin as I remember his soft caressing fingers all along my most sensitive spots. How his fingers trailed from my neck to my chest, my stomach, hips, and between my legs.

"I miss you so much, babe," I whisper to myself, knowing I won't get an answer. Opening my eyes again, I follow the ripples in the water, the wind blowing across the top layer. I rest my forehead against the cold glass, my eyes focused on the water until something catches my eye in the corner of the yard.

Near the wood line, I can see the faintest silhouette of a shadow, unmoving. I squint, trying to make out the form until it starts to move. Lifting my head from the glass, I watch as the form comes closer, coming to the light of the pool. It stops. It's a man, I think. I should be screaming for the guys. This should be terrifying, but I'm perfectly calm. A feeling of peace washes over my entire body, making me feel insanely light.

I watch him.

Unmoving.

Eerily still.

He's staring at me.

"Colson?" I ask, talking to myself and not expecting an answer. I watch the shadow, my skin itching for a response. When I'm about to open the sliding door, I hear him.

"Sweetheart." The faintest whisper filling my ear. My eyes instantly fill with tears so large my vision starts to blur. A sob escapes my throat as I quickly try to wipe away the tears and clutch my coffee mug at the same time. I train my eyes on the Shadow, scared if I lose sight of him, he will disappear.

"Colson," I say again between sobs. This is insane, this can't be Colson, he's gone. It can't be real. I can sense his presence, though. The warmth that always came with him entering a room, the feeling of being weightless yet completely grounded by his love. A sensation of euphoric bliss that only Colson could ever create.

"Focus on me," I hear a whisper, reaching from one ear to the other as if it soared through my ear canal with the wind. A breath of a whisper making my heart race at an impossible speed.

"What?" I ask. Although I know what he said, I want to hear him again. His voice never comes. I ask again, a beg, wanting to hear his voice over and over.

But it never comes.

I'm startled from the window as a pair of footsteps

enter the kitchen, breaking my focus. I turn to see Dean with his arms raised above his head as he stretches through a deep yawn. He doesn't see me as I stand in the darkness of the living room. Turning back to the window, he's gone. The shadow is gone, and my chest feels empty again. Lowering my head, I take a deep breath as Dean suddenly realizes I'm here.

"Shit, baby girl, I didn't see you there." His voice is full of sleep as he makes his way over to me. I give him a small smile, setting my coffee mug on the coffee table and entering his outstretched arms as he wraps me in his cocoon.

"What are you doing awake so early?" he asks me, kissing the top of my head and lifting me into his arms. Dean's large hands cup my ass as he turns and heads back towards the kitchen.

"I could ask you the same thing," I counter, not wanting to admit that my mind is entirely fucked up from training yesterday. I turn my head one last time to the glass door, hoping he may be there, but he's not.

"What are you looking at?" he asks me, following my line of sight.

"Nothing, I was just watching the water." I don't know why I keep Colson's shadow to myself. Maybe because even I know how crazy it would sound if I told him I think I saw a ghost. Or maybe because I want to keep our encounters between us. I kiss the tip of Dean's nose as he sets me on the island and stands between my legs. He stares down at me for a moment, his expression growing somber.

"How are you feeling about today?" My stomach instantly flips at the thought of another session in virtual reality. I don't want to show my fear, though, so I smile at him.

"I'm ready. It's all in the past. I've handled it before, and I can handle it again." Dean doesn't look convinced, his eyes narrow into slits as he continues to stare at me. "I'm fine, Dean, really." Leaning forward, I kiss his neck, generating a growl deep in his throat at my touch. I continue kissing my way from the base of his ear to just above his collarbone. His skin instantly heats beneath my touch, and his abs flex hard every time my lips come down on him.

"Should I stop?" I whisper against his skin. I feel the unmistakable bulge of what my touch is doing to him, pressing firm against my stomach. Threading his fingers through my hair and yanking my head back, he peers down at me, my scalp screaming at the pain of his grasp.

"Don't you fucking dare stop," he growls down at me, his lips brushing mine as he speaks. A sweet smile creeps across my face as I reach for the hem of his sweatpants. Reaching inside, I find his already erect cock as I wrap my fingers around his base and slowly begin to pump up and down. He shutters against my touch and presses harder into my hand as I glide my hand up and down his impressive length.

"Like this?" I tease, as our lips hover over one another. He doesn't answer me. Instead, his lips crash to mine, his hand still firmly pressing against the back of my head as his tongue slips past my lips. Moaning into his mouth, I continue to pump his hard cock, a bead of precum slipping from his tip. Our breathing turns rapid as we consume each other's mouths, licking and sucking, the sound of our lips smacking filling the kitchen.

Dean's hand reaches around my head, his long fingers wrapping around my neck, squeezing ever so softly. Pushing me away by my throat, he leans my body back until I'm lying flat on the cold granite countertop.

"I love this view. My personal buffet, ready for me to devour." Reaching for my sleep shorts, I lift my butt off the counter and allow him to yank them from my legs, my panties following along. Peering down at me, a devilish smile forms across his plump lips. My legs fall to the side, and his eyes lock on my already wet pussy.

"You're glistening for me already, doll. It's like you know how starved I am for you." He leans forward, his lips slowly lapping up my folds, moaning as he takes in my arousal. "So fucking delicious. I can't get enough." His mouth finds my clit, his tongue strong as he licks and flicks my sensitive spot, making my legs twitch beneath his hold. Dean wraps his hands around my thighs, pulling me closer to his face as his mouth continues to devour me. His hot breath against my most sensitive spot ignites a fire in my core.

Arching my back, I put my hands on his head and push him closer to my pussy as my body fights to catch the orgasm that's cresting within me. I don't fight for very long—his deep growl between my legs has me crashing into my orgasm so hard my brain goes fuzzy with the pleasure that soars to my pussy. He continues licking and sucking at my release until I slowly start coming down from the euphoric waterfall. Lifting his face, he licks my release off his lips, desire burning through his gray eyes. He pulls his sweatpants down past his hips, his cock springing free.

Hard and ready.

Pulling me to the edge of the island by my thighs, he lines himself up with my throbbing center, teasing me with his tip as he continues to stare down at me. I'm suddenly so hot, my skin is vibrating with heat. I pull my sleep shirt over my head; the instant sensation of the cold island is like a shockwave as it hits my back. My breasts bob free, and I grab them both, rubbing and massaging them, the heat of Dean's eyes egging me on.

"My dirty little girl, you like touching yourself?" He places a finger over my clit and starts making circular motions before continuing. "Touch yourself here, while I fuck your sweet pussy." With one hand, I continue massaging my breast, but with the other, I obey his command and start making my own circular motions with my two fingers.

"Ughh, Dean, fuck me already." He wastes no more time, thrusting his cock all the way inside me. I gasp at the sudden pain his length creates. The pain is a welcoming sensation as my pussy stretches for him before he pulls out and slams hard inside me again.

"Fuck, doll, you're so tight for me." Dean's fingers are digging into my thighs as he uses them for stability. I close my eyes. "I reveal in the pleasure of my fingers moving faster against my clit as Dean's cock fills me, and the euphoria within me grows once more."

"Look at me while I fuck you." Dean's voice is muffled as my body continues reaching for the pleasure that's soon to crash down on me.

"Look at me, Sloan." His voice is stern, and when I open my eyes, he's glaring down at me, and he's close. "Remember who this pussy belongs to." He slams his body into mine, his cock reaching that spot inside me, and I yell out as my orgasm floods my system, an avalanche of the most beautiful sensation filling me from the inside. Dean reaches his climax as well, his cock twitching inside me as his release fills me up. His body still flexing as he rides out his orgasm, still buried deep inside me.

Leaning his head down to my stomach, he starts kissing along my skin. Soft, peppery kisses cause me to shiver against him as his cock slowly starts to slide out of me. His lips venture up my abdomen and between my breasts, kissing and licking the sheen of sweat until he reaches my chin, giving it a small bite and finally landing on my lips. His hold on my thighs releases as I let my legs fall to the island. I can feel the evidence of his release falling down the insides of my legs, but I don't care. I kiss Dean back as he presses his warm body against mine.

"I love you, baby girl," he says in a whisper, kissing my cheeks, nose, and back to my lips.

"I love you too," I reply, wrapping my legs around his waist as my arms fall around his neck. This is Dean, my gentle giant that fucks me hard but then kisses away the pain of it all.

"Alright, you two, as much as I want to jump in and join you, we have training to do." Everett's tone is soft and joking, but there is no doubt that he would definitely join if we didn't already have a busy day ahead of us.

Pulling away from me, Dean gives me one last kiss on my nose before pulling me into a sitting position and helping me back into my sleep top. He then catches a wet washcloth from Everett and assists in cleaning me up before helping me step into my shorts. What a gentleman.

"Now go get dressed, love. I'll get breakfast started before we head out." Everett slaps my ass as I make my way to the stairs, but before leaving the kitchen, I turn to him.

"Next time, don't wait for an invitation—you're

always welcome." I blow him a kiss over my shoulder before exiting the kitchen.

"For fuck's sake, mate, now I have a hard-on from watching the two of you." Everett chuckles as he admits to Dean, and I can't help the laugh that escapes me. Now I know, all three of them have a thing for watching, apparently.

My dirty, dirty men.

CHAPTER 11

SLOAN

September 16, 2021

What the fuck have we done? After kidnapping the girl, an absolute angel of a girl, we were instructed to bring her to Stone Fortress! Fucking Stone Fortress! What have we done bringing her to that place? Since when has this organization been involved in delivering girls to sex trafficking rings? Something is wrong and the guys agree with me. She won't be there for long; we're getting her back. This was never supposed to happen. We don't do jobs like this. We take out the bad guys, not deliver innocent women to them. We'll get her back, and if anyone touches her before we get there, God save their soul.

I run upstairs and clean myself up a bit from Dean's and my escapades in the kitchen. I jump into the shower, giving myself a quick wash, careful not to get my hair wet. After my two-minute shower, I get dressed in my usual training clothes—jeans and a long-sleeved shirt—before grabbing my tennis shoes and heading back downstairs.

Before reaching the stairs, I stop outside Colson's room, staring at his closed door. Closing my eyes for a second, I remember what he said this morning, or rather the ghost I'm assuming was him.

Focus on me.

Inhaling a deep breath, I repeat this over and over in my head until I can see Colson's image perfectly in my mind.

Focus on me.

Everett was right. I need to focus on a memory that is so strong it drowns out the chaos that will be ensuing around me. Colson, he is my memory, my happiest memory that will guide me through the depths of hell and back to the light.

Focus on me.

"Focus on you," I whisper to myself, inhaling another deep breath before opening my eyes again. My body suddenly feels calmer, lighter, and at ease with what is coming today. As long as I focus on him, my mind will be safe. I will be safe. Straightening my back, I start for the stairs, walking a little bit taller than I was before. His image, his face, his presence will get me through this, I know it.

Everett has made us all his infamous French toast, complete with fresh strawberries and whipped cream on top. My absolute favorite. I take my time with breakfast, enjoying every bite as the three of us sit at the island and silently enjoy our meal. Everett and Dean are just as nervous as I am, and the tension in the room is palpable.

I practice forming his image in my mind with every bite. Reconstructing his golden skin, his toned physique, the way his long blond hair always framed his face, even when he had it pulled back in a bun. His bright smile that always promised mischief. The dimple in his left cheek that would appear only when he tried to hide his devilish grin. The way his golden eyes would lock on mine, causing my knees to go weak with just one look. I can almost feel him, the way his body was a furnace, radiating heat just from being near him. In my mind, I could almost reach out and touch him. This is what he meant when he said focus on me. When I'm focusing on him, nothing else matters around me.

A smile creeps across my face at the perfectly formed image of Colson in my head.

"What are you smiling about, love?" Everett's smooth voice causes me to flinch out of my daydream. My eyes snap to him. I see that both of them have finished their plates, and their eyes are fixated on me. No doubt wondering what the fuck I'm thinking about.

"I'm doing what you said, focusing on a memory." I don't give the details of what this memory is, just the indication that it's a good one and will be of great value to me in the simulation room. A small humming noise comes from Everett, and he nods his head in understanding.

"From here, it looks like you have a pretty solid memory. Don't lose it. Focus on it," Dean says between his sips of coffee.

And I will.

This is how I will succeed in the simulations. I will beat this like I've beaten everything in my life thus far.

Colson is with me.

Finishing breakfast, the three of us clean up our plates and finish getting our bags ready before heading to the Range Rover. I take up the passenger seat as Everett gets in the driver's seat. Dean is stretched out in the back, his laptop resting on his thighs as he starts typing away. As we take off down the driveway, I can feel my heart rate pick up speed as the image of the house fades in the distance. I know this day will only be worse than yesterday.

Each day, the simulations get more and more disturbing and traumatic. So I've been told. Yesterday was just the beginning of my emotional training camp. If yesterday was just the beginning, I can't say I'm not scared shitless for what's to come. Staring out the window, I can feel my mouth turn dry, my jaw is tight from me clenching it so hard, and I fear I might break a tooth.

I reach for my water bottle in the cup holder, pop open the silicone straw, and take a few long sips.

"You'll be okay, baby girl, you are so much

stronger than you know." Everett reaches his hand over, resting it on top of my thigh giving it a small squeeze. I turn to him, looking at the side of his face as his gaze remains on the road. I open my mouth to respond, but nothing comes out. Licking my lips, I try again, but I can't say a word or even form a sentence.

Suddenly, the side of Everett's face starts fading to a blur. The once sharp edges of his jaw have become smoother—softer and more unfocused. Black spots begin speckling my vision, and no matter how much I try to blink away this distortion, it progresses even more. The interior of the vehicle starts to lose its shape, everything mushing together into one giant blob of confusion. I can no longer distinguish between the dashboard, the steering wheel, and the stereo monitor. Everything is now a large pool of colors.

I open my mouth again to ask what the fuck is going on, but again, nothing comes out.

"Just sit back, love, let it take hold of you. We didn't want to stick you again, so we—" Then my hearing goes. I can't hear whatever Everett was about to say, or was that Dean's voice? Everything is a kaleidoscope of colors, and I swear I can see words. Strong hands grab my shoulders, pulling me back to my chair, and I give in. Letting my head rest back on the seat, I close my eyes to the madness. It's happening again. This is my entrance to the simulation. No use in fighting the inevitable.

Let's get this over with.

CHAPTER 12

SLOAN

September 18, 2021

She's here. She's with us, under our roof and safe from the confines of Stone Fortress. She's so unafraid, so calm, so unlike anyone I've ever met. She's been kidnapped again, and she acts as though this is not the worst thing to ever happen to her. Who is this girl? She put up a good fight as the three of us were escorting her to the car, but one girl against three guys is not a fair fight. She accepted the inevitable and came with us. I don't feel bad, because honestly, if she knew what was waiting for her at Stone Fortress, she would be thanking us for retrieving her. Then again, she still has no idea the three of us are the reason she was there in the first place. This should be an interesting conversation when the time comes. I'll leave that to Everett.

. . .

It's bone-chillingly cold here. My skin has tightened to an uncomfortable state as my body tries to hold on to any warmth my body has left. My eyelids are excruciatingly heavy; it's too hard to open them. I want to see where I'm at, but I'm so tired, so drained. Why is it so cold? Inhaling through my nose, a familiar stench invades my nostrils, causing me to freeze. Lying utterly still, I manage to peel open my eyes. The room is spinning, and I can't distinguish if I'm inside or outside. Everything is spinning.

For fuck's sake.

Rubbing my eyes, I try to focus on something, anything, to allow me to figure out where the hell I'm at. When my eyes finally adjust, I recognize my surroundings, and my stomach drops. I'm in the basement. How did I get here? Sitting up off the cold, wet concrete floor, I look down at myself. I'm in nothing but an oversized shirt I remember getting from the thrift store and my panties. Nothing else, no pants, no socks, no shoes, nothing. No wonder I'm freezing. My body is wet from the floor, and the smell of mold mixed with mildew fills the small space.

I remember this place.

It's a small basement, maybe ten by ten, with nothing around but a broken washer and dryer that hasn't been used in years. The overhead light is one exposed light bulb that hangs from a cord attached to the ceiling. It doesn't illuminate much but gives me just enough to see myself as well as the empty room.

There are no windows to give off natural light The small set of five steps consists of old, rotted wood that looks as though the next person to step on will fall right through.

I remember this place.

Standing from my sitting position, I shiver when my feet hit the floor, and a wave of cold shoots up from my feet to my legs and throughout my body. It's so cold. Wrapping my arms around my body, I'm hit with a sharp pain coming from my forearms. Releasing my hold, I look down, examining my arms, and notice the familiar cigar burns my father gave me before bringing me down here. After peppering my skin with cigar burns, my father locked me down here. I can't remember how long it was. All I remember was how cold I was for the entirety of being locked up.

My skin is torched; the skin around the edges of the burns has turned dry and charred. The middle of the burns are still inflamed and red, each one screaming in pain, while some have now started to ooze pus—no doubt infected from this filthy place. I close my eyes and try to recollect this memory. How long was I here for? What happened down here? Is there more torture to come? It's been so long, and I've managed to disassociate from this horrific memory, and now I've forgotten the outcome. I wrap my arms around my body once again, but this time, I am careful not to rub the burns against my wet shirt.

The handle to the door starts to turn, and I stop breathing. The small room echoes with the jiggle of the handle, and whoever is on the other side is having a hard time unlocking the door. Just when I think the person is about to give up, the door violently swings open, crashing into the wall.

My dad.

My stupidly drunk father stands in the doorway, frustration etched across his face from the difficulty of trying to unlock the door. Being drunk makes a simple task much harder to do by the looks of it.

"You're still breathing, huh, kid?" His words slur as he stumbles through the doorway, clutching a bottle of some cheap whiskey. I don't respond. I stand there watching as he takes each step carefully so as not to fall over from his drunken state. With each step, my father becomes more and more illuminated by the small light. When he steps into full view, the wave of this memory comes barreling down on me like a fucking freight train.

My breathing picks up as the memory of this event plays like a movie in my mind. My broken nose, my black eyes, four broken ribs, a dislocated shoulder, and a concussion are all the injuries this man is about to cause me. My eyes start to sting as the realization of the pain to come hits me in full force.

"You think you've learned your lesson now? You're not special, Sloan. Remember that. I've given you everything! A roof over your head, food, a room!

You should be thanking me every fucking day!" The air is knocked from my lungs as my father punches me with all his force straight in my gut. I can't breathe as I crumple to the floor, holding my stomach tight. I try sucking in air, but he pulls me up by my hair and lands another punch. Crack. My nose crunches beneath his fist as blood sprays across my face.

"You should be worshipping me, you little bitch!" I can't remember what I'd done to make him this mad, that is, if I did anything at all. I was always his punching bag when he became belligerent. I was the one constant he could beat on, treat like garbage, and take out all his anger on. I was his escape from his own pain inside.

Another fist lands on my side, and I hear the crack of a rib before I collide with the concrete again. It's like I'm reliving all the pain again. With every punch, every bone that cracks—I can feel it all. A heavy boot comes down on my side as more bones cracking echoes in the small space. How am I here? Tears fall from my eyes as sharp pains shoot through me like electricity. Everything hurts. Everything feels like it's broken. Blow after blow after blow has me wishing I was dead all over again. The attack stops for a moment, allowing me to catch my breath as my father takes a large swig from his whiskey bottle, breathing heavily between sips as if beating me to a pulp is a workout for him. I want to die.

Focus on me.

His voice is so clear, so close, as if he's lying right next to me on the floor.

Focus on me, Sloan.

Colson.

Closing my eyes hard, I see golden skin, hazel eyes, long blond hair, and one dimple. One heart-wrenching dimple. Another kick to my side has the image disappearing as quickly as it came. I moan as the aches of my ribs make it hard to breathe.

Focus on me! the voice says again, but louder this time.

I open my eyes and see a boot coming towards me again, but before it can reach me, I roll to my other side, narrowly avoiding another bone-crushing blow.

"You fucking coward!" I hear my father's voice boom through the room as his boot meets the concrete.

Focus on me.

Colson, Colson, Colson. I say his name over and over in my head as I find the strength to stand up, the pain travels all over my body. I make it to my feet just in time for my father to punch me once again across my cheek. I stumble but don't fall. I remain on my feet, unsteady but still standing.

Golden skin, hazel eyes, bright smile. He's with me. I can feel him. The sudden gust of cold air dances through my hair in a quick burst. Colson. Standing as tall as I can manage with my broken ribs, I stare deep into my father's black eyes.

"Cowards are people who choose to beat up on the vulnerable. From where I'm standing, it looks to me like you're the coward. You fucking piece of shit." I have never in my life spoken to my father in such a brazen manner before, but something about this moment feels different. I feel different.

This isn't real.

I tell myself this can't be real. I've already lived this moment in my life. This can't be real. The look my father gives me is that of a starving bear after he's hibernated all winter. Anger. Frustration. Rage screams through his hollow eyes, and I know at this moment I'm going to survive this. I'm bleeding, bruised, and broken, but I will not let this man take anything more from me than he already has. Fuck him.

"You think you're brave, do you? I'll teach you what it's like to be brave. Jerry, Michael, come down here. I've got something for ya!" Jerry and Michael? As I stand there staring at my father, both his friends come up from behind, each giving a devilish grin as they approach me from each side.

No. No. I won't let this happen again. Not now. As the two men close in on me, I back up with each of their steps until my back is against the wall. Greedy, calloused hands grab my arms as they hold me still. Thrashing and kicking against their holds, I see my father approaching me with a cigar tucked between his lips.

Closing my eyes tight, I try to awaken myself from this nightmare. Like a lucid dream, I know this can't be real. Opening my eyes again, I see my father closing in on me fast. I continue thrashing and kicking, trying to free my broken body but getting nowhere as the hands on me grow tighter. A puff of smoke slinks its way through my nostrils, burning as it invades my sinus cavity. My eyes begin to water from the sudden intrusion, my legs becoming heavy as I kick nothing but the air in front of me. My father is just out of my reach, and my fear quickly subsides to inevitable defeat as I slowly stop the fight, knowing what's coming.

I still beneath their grasp, inhaling deeply as I try to steady my racing heart that's thumping hard inside my chest. The heat of the cigar is mere centimeters from my skin when I close my eyes, and I stiffen my muscles, awaiting the pain. As I close my eyes, I see him. Golden skin, sun-kissed blond hair, and hazel eyes. He calls my name.

Sloan. Want to go for a swim? His voice is quiet, barely a whisper. I don't answer. I just squeeze my eyes shut tighter and focus on the figure in my mind.

Sloan, you can wear the bikini I love, and we can play truth or dare again. My eyes begin to sting. The image of Colson is so vivid in my mind it's like he's actually standing in front of me.

"Is this going to hurt?" I whisper, eyes cemented shut as I continue to wait for the burning of my flesh that's yet to come.

They can't hurt you unless you let them. Unless you show them, you're no longer afraid of them. Show them who've you become, sweetheart. Fight. As clear as the image of Colson was, he quickly fades away. He's gone and I'm left chasing the phantom of a beautiful soul that continues to save me, even in the afterlife.

A feeling of pure adrenaline and strength takes over as the power of my self-preservation takes hold of me. I open my eyes just as my father presses his cigar into my forearm. The fire seeps through layers of my skin, and I can feel the pain all over again. Except this time, I don't let them see how much it truly hurts. Tensing my muscles, I harden my face, eyes dark with murderous intent. Years of rage, built up as high as the pyramids, are about to come crashing down on these three putrid human beings.

My father lifts his cigar from my now charred skin, looking at me as I stare back into his beady eyes. His face is twisted in confusion as he waits for my reaction, but I don't give him one. His brows are pinched tight as he looks me over—a woman transformed into something other than his once weak daughter.

"You smell that, boys?" My father inhales a deep breath, as the smell of freshly burned flesh fills the air, but before they can respond, I answer for them.

"It's the smell of decaying flesh and bones piled high. Your limbs scattered across the floor, eyeballs tacked to the wall, tongues ripped from your throats, and blood pooling around my feet. Lots and lots of blood. It's what I'm going to do to you three in roughly eight seconds." The room goes silent. The only audible sound is my heartbeat thumping in my ears as I create the most gruesome death imaginable in my mind.

I countdown aloud, as I watch my father's face go from confusion to curiosity to the slightest hint of fear in a flash. An evil grin forms on my face, enjoying the flood of emotions playing across his face as I continue counting.

"Five."

"Four."

"Three."

"Two."

I tense every muscle in my body as I prepare to dislodge myself from their grasp, my scene of escape playing on a loop in my head. As I'm about to say my last number, a blinding light assaults my eyes, and I'm forced to close them as the sting of the brightness becomes too much. The hold on me begins to subside, and my equilibrium starts going haywire as the room morphs from a stale basement to a sterile white room occupied by nothing and no one, except for myself.

I'm no longer the victim of my father and his friends. I'm standing alone breathing rapidly as I look down at my forearm and no longer see an angry burn but rather an old, scarred circle; evidence that this moment truly did happen. Many, many years ago.

I hear a door click open. Lifting my face, I see

Arno's smiling face beaming at me. He's clapping his hands at me, the loud echoing of his large hands slapping against one another fills the space as he makes his way towards me.

"What a fucking show, little one. To say I'm impressed would be a serious fucking understatement." His voice booms through the room, as I continue to stand utterly still. He reaches me and bends down enough to see into my eyes, his hands resting on either side of my shoulders. My breathing has evened out, but something deep in my chest has me cemented into place. I feel as though a wave of black water has crashed into my soul, taking over as it soars through my body in a tsunami of darkness.

"Hey, little one, are you okay?" I can hear Arno's voice, but my mind doesn't send the signals I need to my mouth so I can respond to him. Instead, I nod once as I lift my eyes to his. My face remains stoic as he peers down at my zombie-like form.

"It's over now. You're free. Look at me, Sloan." His voice is laced with concern as he shakes my shoulders in an effort to break me from the trance I've fallen into.

"Say something, Sloan." Hardening my eyes on Arno, I open my mouth a moment as I inhale a long shallow breath.

"I'll never be free of the chaos that is my life, Arno. It's a black mold penetrating my soul, creating me into this monster until the only thing I want to do is kill someone." His eyebrows rise at my last statement. An expression of uncertainty about how to handle my new attitude creeps across his face. Just as he's opening his mouth to respond, I stop him.

"I will kill someone, Arno. And you're going to help me."

CHAPTER 13

EVERETT

"She's lost to it. The memory was too much, and she's already become blind to the rage that's been festering inside her for her whole life." Arno fills us in on Sloan's session from this morning. Dean and I were escorted out of the viewing room. The second her father started hitting our girl, the rage inside of us boiled over to a whole new level. Stefan, Jei, and Arno had to physically restrain us before we could hit the termination button to free Sloan from her nightmare. Under no circumstance are we allowed to interfere with sessions, no matter how disturbing they may be.

The sound of his fist cracking across her face and seeing the blood gushing from her nose had me seeing red, and not from her blood. I wanted to kill someone at that moment. I wanted to insert myself into her memory so I could rip apart her father piece by piece, while enjoying the sounds of his agony. I felt helpless, and my chest was cracking apart as she continued to endure blow after blow. No one hurts what's mine. No one.

After being restrained and removed from the room, Dean and I made a pact that we would hunt down her father and torture him in more ways than he ever did to Sloan. He will beg for death after what we plan to do to him.

Arno, Dean, and I are currently in the viewing room. Sloan was escorted from the simulation room by Arno, but she insisted that she needed to shower. After leaving her at the locker rooms, Arno immediately came to fill us both in on her current state of mind.

"I'm not sure if she's just in shock still and will soon break from her trance or if she completely shut off her emotional connection to her trauma," Arno continues, his face etched with pain as he describes our girl. "She was blank coming out of the simulation. It was as though she knew the whole thing was fake and fought back against her father, altering the course of the memory entirely. Almost like she was in a lucid dream, once the pain became too much, she realized it was all a dream." He stops talking, beginning to pace the room as he takes a few deep breaths.

"You think she created a barrier between her emotions rather than trying to control them?" I ask him, watching as he scratches his head while continuing to take small steps back and forth. He doesn't answer me though, he turns to me, placing his hands in his trouser pockets and gives me a shrug. Dean lets out a heavy breath as he curses to himself. His large frame puffing out as his anger continues to fester within him.

"She looked me dead in my eyes and told me she was going to kill someone, and that I was going to help her," Arno speaks in barely a whisper, his shoulders curling in on themself as he speaks. "I have to admit, mate, I'm not sure she is ready to advance in her training after this one. Not until you two can bring her back from the fire she's thrown herself in."

"I fucking knew something like this would happen. We shouldn't have agreed on this, Everett. We're going to lose the girl we fell in love with," Dean spits in an angry growl as he, too, starts pacing the room. Letting out a heavy sigh, I comb my hair back with my hands. The threat of a migraine begins to throb from the uncertainty of what to do next. Racking my brain, I'm at a complete loss as to how to help her. If she truly wants to be a Shadow, these are the steps she'll need to take to succeed. However, Dean is right, I'm not willing to lose the girl we love so she can become something she's not.

The click of the door has my attention snapping to Sloan as she enters the room looking freshly showered. Her hair is still damp, and she's wearing her usual jeans and a gray long-sleeved shirt that hugs her petite frame. Her face is unreadable, but she doesn't look distressed or pained as she makes her way over to the three of us.

"What's next?" she says, as she stops beside me, looking at the three of us one by one. I'm shocked and unsure of what to say. The room is quiet as we all share a glance before landing back on Sloan. Dean places himself in front of her, placing his hands on her shoulders while peering down at her. She stays still, only lifting her neck to return Dean's stare. It's almost as if this isn't Sloan at all. She moves on autopilot with no emotions playing across her beautiful face, making it damn hard to determine where her head is at.

"That's it for today. No more simulations." Dean's tone is harsh as he lifts his eyes to me, almost as if to say that's final. Looking down at Sloan's face, I can see her eyebrows pinch together at Dean's dictation. She looks almost mad, an expression I was not expecting.

"Wait, why? This is what I need to do to move forward with training. I can do this, I'm fine. Put me back in, let me get this over with sooner rather than later," she barks as she backs away from Dean's hold. She frantically looks up to me and then to Arno, who is standing slightly perpendicular to Dean. "Tell them Arno, I'm fine. I realized I was in a dream and controlled my emotions. Even you said how impressed you were, tell them." Her eyes are hard on Arno waiting for his response, but all he does is give her a sympathetic smile.

"There's a difference between controlling your emotions and eliminating them entirely." My voice is soft but stern as I peer down at her crystal-blue eyes. I still can't read her; her face is blank as she comprehends what I'm saying. I'm about to say something else, but Sloan speaks first.

"Okay, then tomorrow." With that, she turns and makes her way to the door.

"Where are you going?" I call out, causing her to halt before she reaches for the handle.

She doesn't turn to face me, she says over her shoulder, "To the gym. I need to hit the bag, or run, or something." She fumbles over her words, not really sure what she needs to do at this point. As she leaves the three of us in the viewing room, I'm speechless for the first time in my life and unsure how to fix the problem we undoubtedly created.

CHAPTER 14

SLOAN

October 10, 2021

I'm falling for this girl, and not just me, Dean and Everett are too. She's an enigma. Not how I would imagine a girl who's been tortured her whole life to be. She's witty and fun, she doesn't let her past define her, she just lives for the moment. She's incredibly strong and resilient. She's conquered more in her short life than most women would in a lifetime. As much as the three of us are falling for her, I think she may be falling for us as well. There is something off about this whole situation of us kidnapping her and bringing her to Stone Fortress, and it's making me distrust anyone within the organization right now. I've brought this journal home with me, which is a huge violation, but something inside me feels uneasy about leaving this at headquarters where essentially anyone can read it. No, I've brought it home, and this is where it will stay. At first, I hated this journal and writing my thoughts down in a *stupid book. Now I find it helpful, like a brain dump onto paper, allowing me to clear my mind.*

I'm scared. Or rather, I think I'm scared. I know I should be scared. I did everything Dean made me promise I wouldn't do. Something happened to me in that last simulation. I felt it and can still feel it now as I run on the treadmill. I feel nothing—totally numb and indifferent to anything that has ever happened to me. At first, I welcomed the feeling of not feeling anything at all, but now I feel stuck. I think about my parents and everything they put me through, and I should feel angry, but I don't. I think about Colson and never being able to step into his embrace again, and I should be heartbroken, but I'm not.

My heart and chest feel like the dentist coated my whole insides with their numbing agent. I can't break through the paralyzing feeling that's latched onto my muscles to allow any emotion to come in. My brain wants to feel, it wants to express how these situations have molded me into the person I am today, but the signals are not being interpreted properly within my nervous system. My brain is telling me I'm scared, but I can't feel the pang of anxiety that a racing heart would create when one is scared. I know what emotions I want to feel, I'm just stuck. I'm stuck in this perpetual state of nothingness, and I fear I won't be able to escape from it.

Glancing down at the treadmill, I see I've run four-

and-a-half miles and I'm barely even breathing hard. I slow my pace to a walk, trying to slow down the chaos within and trying to focus on my brain to heart communication. Something I've never done before—and yes—it is as hard as it sounds.

After walking for another five minutes, I hit *stop* on the treadmill. Once the track stops moving, I sit on the edge of the machine. Resting my elbows on my knees, I let my head fall towards the floor. What happened to me in that simulation? It was just like Dean said—a switch inside me flipped, and now I'm stuck and can't turn it back on. Just another thing my father and his lowlife piece of shit friends took from me. I want to feel mad. I want to feel rage consume me as I direct that feeling towards my father. But I feel nothing.

The gym door opens, and I look up to see Dean. His face is hard and set on me as he makes his way towards me. Sitting directly in front of me on the opposite treadmill, he leans his arms atop his knees, making it so our faces are inches apart. I look away from him, not wanting to meet his eyes.

"Look at me, Sloan." Dean's tone is low and deep, giving me chills as his words fill the gym. I don't obey his command. I continue to look towards the floor; his intense stare is too much for me right now.

"Look at me." His volume rises just slightly, but still, I don't listen. I hear him sigh a deep breath right before his fingers take hold of my chin and force my face to his. I'm not scared of him; I don't want to discuss what is happening to me.

"You lied to me, baby girl." I freeze at this comment. As if I could have controlled the outcomes of that simulation any more than I already had. How dare he accuse me of lying?

"Oh, yeah? How did I do that?" My tone is even, almost sounding bored with this conversation already. Dean's eyebrows pinch together, my comment causing his face to darken in that familiar anger that sweeps over him in the blink of an eye, as he releases my chin.

"As if you don't remember. You promised you wouldn't lose yourself in this training. You promised you wouldn't lose the real Sloan to the chaos of your past." I listen to his words, letting them fill me up as I try to feel guilt, sadness, rage, anything. But nothing fills me up. I sit up straighter, not really sure what to say, or how to explain any of this to him. I take a few deep breaths, closing my eyes as I do, and try to muster up the logical explanation for what is happening inside me.

"I have no idea what to say, Dean. I'm just as confused as you. One minute I feel everything. My father's cigar burning into my skin, his fist cracking against my jaw, the hands of his friends restraining me so tightly I can feel the bruises forming beneath my skin. Then, just like that, it was all gone. Everything went blank, my insides were swept clean of any and all nerve endings. I lost it all. I felt no pain. It was nice," I whisper that last bit. I truly liked the feeling of not feeling anything in that moment, but when the simulation was over, that numbness stayed with me.

Dean's stare is hot on my skin as I fiddle with my fingers, not knowing what to say next or what to do. His warm hands slip through my fingers, breaking my nervous fidgeting and hold my fingers in his hands. His touch is hard as he squeezes my hands a little too hard. I stare at our connection, wanting to feel the electricity of his touch, but it never comes. It's at this moment I realize the extent of switching off your emotions. I snap my eyes to his, wondering if I lost the connection between us.

I know I love him, and I love Everett. There's no questioning that, but have I lost the chemistry that's formed between us whenever they touch me? Have I lost the feeling of being full, of being loved, of being wanted? Without thinking any further, I grab Dean's face in my hands and kiss him with so much force our teeth click together as I desperately try to ignite the fire I fear is now being smothered.

Dean snakes his hands around my back and hoists me into his lap. Straddling his waist, I continue to kiss him, our lips moving in sync with each other as I devour him. Grinding my hips against his rapidly swelling cock, I continue moving my hips as the ache between my legs demands more friction. If I can feel the pleasure building deep in my core, that has to be a good sign that I'm not completely lost, right?

Slipping my hands up his shirt, I scratch my

fingers down his defined chest and over every crease of his abdomen until I reach the hem of his pants. A deep groan escapes his mouth, his whole body tightening to my touch.

"Fuck, baby girl, keep going," he says into my mouth as I grab the hem of his shirt and rip it over his head. He raises his arms up to help free himself of his shirt before he threads his fingers through my hair, gripping tight as he brings my face back to his. My scalp is screaming at the hold he has on me, but I welcome the sting. I need to feel something, even if that is pain.

"Harder," I whisper. He obliges and pulls my hair, tilting my head back as he starts licking along my neck, stopping to kiss the sensitive spot right below my ear. He nips my earlobe gently, but I need more.

"Harder." This time I say it a little louder, making sure he knows how much I want his dominance right now. Suddenly, a sharp pain shoots down my shoulder and to my fingers as Dean sinks his teeth into the top of my shoulder, causing me to scream out.

"Yes, yes, do it again!" I need this. I need him to hurt me so I can distinguish the feeling of pain. I need him to help me flip the switch inside me.

"You want me to hurt you, baby?" he asks, his tone curious as his mouth hovers over my collarbone. My pussy is throbbing—the friction of his jeans against my clit is not enough. I need more; I need his cock to fill me up and force its way inside me. I need him to hurt me.

"Yes, punish me, hurt me, make me feel some-thing, Dean." He pauses a moment as the realization of what's happening registers in that split second.

"I fucking knew this was going to happen." Dean sounds angry, and not his normal angry, but the anger he felt when I was kidnapped, or when I was being tortured by Van, or when Colson died. Without another word, Dean throws me off his lap and stands up in an instant. I'm sitting on the treadmill, leaning back on my elbows while Dean towers over me.

"You want me to hurt you, love? Then let's go somewhere where I can do it properly." Dean doesn't let me respond. Instead, he grabs my arm with one hand and my waist with the other, and he lifts me over his shoulder and stocks to the gym door.

"Where are we going?" I ask, but he doesn't answer me. It doesn't take long for me to realize he is taking me to the women's locker room. He kicks the door open and spins us around to flip the lock of the handle before setting me down on my feet. Turning to face me, his eyes dark as night as he stares down at me.

"I'd be lying if I said this didn't happen to all of us during the simulations. We all eventually lost ourselves to the madness and flipped the switch so we didn't have to deal with it anymore. But with you, you promised me you wouldn't, and now look. I have to hurt you in hopes that will bring you back to the light. Pain is arguably the most triggering emotion we have. When we feel it too much, we take drastic measures in hopes of stopping the pain. Do you want me to hurt you, Sloan, because you no longer feel the desire you once had for me? Don't fucking lie to me, either." I hadn't realized Dean was walking towards me until my back was flush against the wall. He's now looking down at me, heat radiating off his body and anger evident in his posture.

Is he right, though? Do I want him to hurt me because I've lost my lust for him and Everett?

"I—I don't know. I just need to feel something. I need you to help me, Dean. Help bring me back. Please," I beg as I lift my arms and rest them on his abdomen.

"I can't feel anything right now, and it's numbing. I don't want to not feel. Help me, Dean." His eyes soften as I plea with him to do something—hurt me, fuck me hard, strangle me for fuck's sake—just do something to fix this black hole of utter nothing that's taking hold of every inch of my being.

Just as I'm lowering my head, about to accept defeat, Dean's hands spin my body around and push me firmly into the wall. The heat of his body against mine is so hot, like when you stand too close to a fire and the heat waves burn you.

"You need to remember, Sloan, you asked for this. This will hurt." I want to feel scared, but at this moment I still don't. I need this from him. I need this to hurt. My jeans are suddenly ripped down my legs, along with my panties, as my entire backside is exposed to him. I can feel the slickness between my legs growing as he grabs the back of my long-sleeve and pulls it just enough so it's no longer touching my back. I expected him to pull it off me, but the sound of metal clicking has me wondering what he's doing. A slicing sound tears through the air, followed by my shirt hanging off my arms in two pieces.

"Now, take it off," he growls, stepping back from me so I can remove the fabric from my chest. I take it off, letting it fall to the floor. The only thing left is my bra, but he makes quick work of that. Unlatching the bra, he pulls the straps down both my arms, and goosebumps prickle my skin. Dean's lips brush my ear as he helps me out of my bra, and I close my eyes to the sensation.

"Now, bend over and hold on to the wall. This will hurt." My body is trembling. Normally, I would be feeling nervous, anxious, or curious about what he's going to do. My body is clearly reacting to his demands, but my brain is still in its zombie state. Quickly, I bend over, exposing my wet cunt to him.

"What are you going to do?" I ask, turning my head to see him unfastening his jeans and freeing his thick cock as he begins to stroke it up and down. He doesn't answer me. He firmly grabs the back of my head, turning it towards the wall once again.

"Don't move." I stay still, as much as I can, as my body trembles. A warm hand glides up my ass, massaging my cheek hard as he squeezes it in his hand, no doubt causing it to bruise. He snakes his other hand around my waist, laying it flat against my stomach. Slowly, he slides his hand lower, past my belly button and to the apex of my pussy. He stops there, his hand hovering over my aching clit—the throb is becoming too much, and the desire for him to touch me grows. I moan, arching my back as his cock slowly presses against my ass.

"I'm going to make it hurt so good, you'll never have to question your desire for me again." With that, he dips his fingers into my pussy, the sudden pressure heating me instantly. As he slowly starts swirling his fingers in my pleasure, his thumb presses against my hole, swirling around, causing a sensation I'm not familiar with. Dean slides his fingers between my folds, spreading the evidence of my arousal as he reaches my hole and starts slowly pressing a finger inside me. It hurts, yes, but it's a pain that you want more of.

"Ugh, Dean," is all I can manage to say. He continues working my backside with one hand as the other squeezes my hip so hard it causes my abdomen to flex against his grasp. As he slips his finger inside my hole, a sharp pain shoots through me like an electric current, causing me to gasp.

"Relax, baby girl. You're doing so good." Dean continues spreading my arousal from my dripping pussy to my ass, preparing me for what's to come. Releasing my hip, I hear him spit into his palm as he works his cock and my backside simultaneously. I'm breathing rapidly at this new type of pleasure; I'm not prepared when the tip of his cock presses against my hole just enough to slide the head inside. The mangled scream that escapes my mouth is truly demonic as the pain of his cock entering inside my tight hole has me seeing stars.

"Tell me, baby girl, what are you feeling right now?" I try to catch my breath and register exactly what he's asking me, but all I can say is, "I feel you." He pushes his cock a little further, the sharp pain increasing.

"Wrong. What are you feeling right now?" he asks again. Dean's hand is back on my hip, squeezing me hard enough where I can't move. I try to register what I'm feeling, what he wants to hear from me, but I'm blank. I'm so focused on his cock slowly pressing inside me that I can't think of an answer.

"I remember when I first saw you at Stone Fortress, I hated you. I didn't want to get involved with anything that wasn't our business." His cock slips in another centimeter. "Then we brought you home, and we made you our business quicker than I anticipated." Releasing my hip, his hand comes down hard on my ass, the sharp sting of his hand slapping my skin causing another scream from my mouth.

"Then every incident after getting you home had me so confused and at war with my emotions. I didn't know how to interpret what was happening to me. It would have been easy to turn it all off, of course." His cock is now halfway inside me. "But that would have been the bitch thing to do, the easy way out. Is that what you're doing, taking the easy way? I knew you couldn't handle this job—I knew you'd bitch out and take the easy road."

Slap. Another crack to my ass.

"If you think asking me to hurt you will miraculously flip your switch, then that shows me you have no control over your emotions, or worse, yourself."

Slap.

"Colson would be so disappointed." With that one comment, I'm seeing red. I'm ready to turn around and face this prick for daring to say such a thing when he forces his cock fully inside me. The pain radiates throughout my entire body. The pain ignites a fire in my core, the sharpness mixing with the sting of his invasion taking over me. I welcome the pain, feeling it as it racks through my body, filling every hole inside until the only thing I feel is the pain.

"So, fucking tight, baby," he groans, his body flush against my ass, his cock still fully seated inside me. "Maybe Colson wouldn't be disappointed—you're taking me so well." Red flashes through my vision once again, and I push my ass back against him until I'm able to release myself from his cock. Spinning around, I give him a death-glare at Dean, rage now taking the place of the pain as my blood starts to boil hot.

"You don't get to talk about him like that!" I yell, and I see the side of his lip start to curl into what looks to be amusement. "You fucking bastard!" I get in his face, sweat starting to form along my hairline.

"Are you mad, baby? Did I take it too far?" His

tone is condescending and full of sarcasm as he steps towards me. I put my hands to his chest, ready to push him back, but his hands clamp over my wrists, making me immobile. He pulls me into his face, his nose a mere millimeter from mine as his dark eyes peer down at me.

"What else do you want to feel? We've got pain, anger—how about lust next? My personal favorite." He quickly lets my wrists go and grabs my ass with both of his hands, lifting me as if I weighed nothing. Wrapping my legs around his waist, he slams my back against the wall, his lips claiming mine in a searing kiss. Dean's lips are soft, yet so powerful he leads this kiss, manipulating mine just the way he wants them. He pulls away from my mouth, and I'm suddenly empty again.

"Every day, every hour, every minute, every fucking second of the day I'm thinking of you, baby. Kidnapping you was the best thing to happen to me, because it brought you to me. You'll forever want me. Your desire for me will never disappear because I will spend the rest of my life making sure you feel me in every way possible." The anger that quickly took hold of me subsides as Dean's confession swirls through my head. I'm speechless.

My whole body begins to feel like a volcano of aches, pains, warmth, serenity, euphoria, and bliss. Every emotion that was once shut down now comes at me in full force. I can feel it in my blood. My veins are pumping so hard as my head tries desperately to sort out the emotions, but they are coming too fast. My brain feels like it's going to explode. My breathing picks up and my vision starts to go cloudy. I can hear Dean saying something, but I can't understand his words. Everything sounds so far away, as if I'm standing at the end of a football field and Dean is at the opposite end.

"What's happening?" I ask, and all I can do is hold on to Dean's shoulders as tight as I can as this atomic bomb is going off inside me.

CHAPTER 15

DEAN

"There you are, love," I whisper to her, but the look on her face says she can't hear a word I'm saying. I pull her into my chest, her arms instinctively wrapping around my neck as she squeezes me tight. The flood of emotions coursing through her small body is no doubt beating her up from the inside out. When we fail to acknowledge the emotions we have, we pack them in a black box that's impenetrable unless you know how to unlock them. I've been in her shoes, I've felt what she's feeling, and it's frustrating but also scary as hell when everything is unleashed at once.

I knew what I needed to do to get her back even though it was going to hurt me as well—it needed to be done. I needed to bombard her with every emotion I could in the shortest span of time. Yes, it's painful, but it's one of the only ways I know how to bring someone back from the empty room she's placed herself in.

She trembles in my arms, the kaleidoscope of feelings starting to internally combust inside her. She needs to focus on one emotion at a time; she needs to grab hold of one of them and allow herself to feel all of it. I grab her ass and lift her just enough so I can line my swollen cock up with her entrance. If she can't focus and grab hold of one emotion, I will choose for her. I don't want her to feel any more pain, so I slowly push the head of my dick into her warm, slick heat. My abdomen tightens, the pleasure instantly hitting my lower belly, and I let out a deep growl as my fingers flex harder on her ass.

She's stopped shaking, the sudden invasion of my cock bringing her focus to me with a sudden gasp.

"That's right, baby girl, come back to me." Her eyes start to adjust on my face, her crystal-blue eyes no longer looking cloudy or miles away. She's slowly coming down from the tsunami. Pleasure, lust, love is what I want her to feel right now. I want her to remember why our emotions are what make us humans. I push my cock inside her deeper, her pussy clenching around me as she moves her hips closer to me, chasing that high of being completely full. With one last slow thrust, our hips meet, and my cock twitches inside her from her warmth.

"What are you feeling now?" I whisper to her, our lips brushing together as I speak. She rests her forehead on mine, her arms tightening around my neck.

Her breathing is evening out as we stay connected, our bodies perfect molds fitting together like puzzle pieces.

"I-I feel—I feel you. I feel warm, full, I feel loved." With those words I pull fully out of her—the sudden absence of her pussy makes me instantly want more. I thrust myself inside her once again. Her moan is music to my ears.

"Don't leave me like that again, baby girl. I can't lose you too." I pull her away from the wall and she removes my clothes with lightning speed before I pick her back up and seat myself inside her once more. I carry her to the Jacuzzi that's located in the corner of the locker room. Kissing her soft lips as I step up the small steps and slowly lower us into the warm water until I'm sitting on the ledge beneath the water. I keep her plastered to me, my cock not leaving her tight pussy as she straddles her legs on either side of my thighs.

Giving her one last kiss, I pull away from her face and look deeply into her eyes.

"There you are," I say, her expression calm and somber as she gently scratches her nails across my scalp. "I'm so sorry, Dean." Her voice is small and barely audible, but I can see her pain when a lone tear slides from her eye and down her cheek. I catch the tear with my tongue and lick it away, the saltiness spreading across my tastebuds.

"Don't apologize. This is what's expected from training. It's different for everyone, but we all lose touch with our emotions at least once with this shit. You're not the first and definitely not the last. I won't let you fall like that again." More tears form in her eyes, and this time when they fall, I kiss each one away.

"I love you, Dean." Her voice is a punch to my heart every time she utters that four-letter word. Never in my life did I imagine a woman ever say that she loves me, but fuck, am I glad it's her.

"I love you more, baby girl." She lifts herself from my lap but then slowly returns as my cock slides in and out of her. I tilt my head back—the sudden calmness of our energy and the pleasure of our bodies moving together feel like perfect bliss as she moves up and down against me. Small moans slip from her mouth as she finds her clit and starts making circular motions with her fingers.

"Good girl," I breathe. "Cum all over my dick." My cock tightens as the pleasure builds inside me. I watch her as she drops her head back, her fingers working herself into a frenzy. Her pussy clenches around me so tightly, my vision starts going black. My whole body flexes as I crash so hard into my orgasm, my head falls to her chest as the waves of pleasure crash through me. She lets out a scream as she finds her pleasure, her body convulsing on top of me, her hips grinding and rolling across my pelvis. I grab her hips, squeezing them gently and holding her tightly to my cock as I spill everything inside of her.

We sit with our foreheads pressed together as we

slowly even out our breaths. I grab her face with one of my hands, snaking my long fingers into her hair and holding her still.

"I'm so proud of you, love," I say in a breathy whisper.

"I love you too, Dean."

––––––––

Following the Jacuzzi, Sloan and I shower together. I take my time washing her long blond hair and then her body. She grabs a washcloth, adds soap, and works it into a lather before washing my body. We stay in the shower longer than we need to. The sound of the water is the only noise filling the locker room. It's peaceful and exactly what she needs. Going from the chaos that was once her emotions raging war inside her body and mind, to the serenity of the water droplets hitting the tile being her form of quiet. It's exactly what she needs.

We finish our shower, both of us grabbing a fresh towel and drying off before we find our clothes. As we head to the door, Sloan grabs my wrist, stopping me before I am able to touch the door handle. Turning around, I look down at her; she appears a million times better than when she exited the simulation. The warmth in her cheeks has returned, her body is less stiff and more relaxed, and her eyes—fuck, her eyes are so beautiful—a crystal blue that brightens as she looks right into my soul.

"Thank you, Dean, for saving me. Again." Her eyes say it all—she was scared. Scared of losing a battle against herself. I know the feeling all too well. Leaning into her, I cup her face in my hands and press my lips to hers. She presses her lips hard into mine, her apology extending to her actions.

"Please don't apologize. None of this should be happening to you in the first place. We are the ones that forever need to be apologizing to you. Now come, they are probably wondering where the hell we are." I chuckle at that last comment, but if I know Everett and Arno like I know I do, they both already know exactly what we've been up to.

CHAPTER 16

SLOAN

October 18, 2021

Who wants this girl dead? Why? She's perfect, utterly perfect. She's survived a fucked-up past, escaped the abuse, built a life of her own, and done nothing, absolutely nothing, to justify others wanting her dead. I don't understand. We are missing something. We have to be. Who wants this girl dead, and why? What makes this girl desired enough to be eliminated? Does she know why? Everett, Dean, and I have been racking our brains trying to piece everything together, but there seems to be a massive hole in all this. Until we're able to figure something out, she stays with us, in our house, under our protection.

Walking hand in hand with Dean down the hallway and towards the lounge room, I can hear Everett and Arno talking. Their voices are muffled and when

Dean opens the door, they both go silent. Their eyes find mine as we both step through the entryway. A sudden pang of anxiety pools in my stomach as the silence becomes too much for me.

"Somebody, please say something. This silence is deafening," I say to the room, not looking at any of them in the face. Taking a seat on one of the sofas, they all follow my lead. Dean immediately takes the seat beside me as Everett and Arno sit on the sofa opposite us. I fold my hands in my lap, fiddling with my fingers nervously before I break the silence once more.

"Listen, I know what you guys are thinking, and I'm here to tell you I'm fine. I lost myself, yes, but Dean helped bring me back. I'm fine now and would like to continue my training." There's a long pause in the room as Everett's gaze weighs heavily on my face. My cheeks redden as his assessment of me is clear. He doesn't want this to continue. He doesn't want me to continue. I shift my eyes to Arno—the heat of Everett's glare is too much for me at the moment. Arno's gaze is on me, his expression more somber, but there's also a sliver of concern in the way he's pinching his eyebrows together. I don't bother looking at Dean. I know he never wanted me to go through with this training, and after today, I'm sure he's still standing strong with his opinion.

"I think she can handle herself, mates. She can do this. She should continue." Dean's voice was the last one I expected to speak up or defend my decision on the matter. Now I do look at Dean. The side of his face is set and hard as he stares between Everett and Arno, awaiting their response.

"Listen, mate, she doesn't need to do this." Everett's tone is stern, the look in his eyes displaying how much he doesn't want to have this discussion.

"She'll be better protected once she completes her training. You know this, Everett." I don't look at Dean as he addresses Everett, I just keep my face neutral when all I want to do is tell Everett how much I do need this. I need this to heal myself, to prove that I can overcome all the bullshit that's torn me down year after year. I can stand on my own two feet and not rely on others to ensure my safety. I can handle myself and live a life without fear. Before either one of them can speak again, I interrupt.

"I do need this, Everett," I say, not entirely meaning to, but the words slip out. His emerald glare lands on me, his eyes pleading with me to stop all this and allow them to handle those who are after me. "I need this, to prove to myself I'm strong. I can survive with all this fucked up shit that's happening around us. I need to prove to myself I'm not the trauma that's been plaguing my soul my entire life. In the simulation today, I felt powerful towards the end. Although I lost myself for a moment, I also found a piece of me that's been hiding in the shadows for far too long. She escaped and finally stood up for herself in that basement." I stand from the sofa, my blood running hot as I explain my reasoning, something I never thought I'd have the courage to do. "When I was in that room, I did what you told me to do. I held onto a memory, a moment in time to help me through. You want to know what that memory was?" I pause, my eyes drifting between the three of them. "It was Colson," I choke out, his name on my tongue tasting sweet—I crave him day after day.

"I saw him in my head, the way his skin glowed, his wild, untamed hair, the way his hazel eyes brought me such peace. I knew he would help me through that moment." My voice shakes as I continue. "I see him everywhere. Call me crazy, but I swear he's here with me, helping me every step of the way." I close my eyes. "I can hear his voice sometimes. Short little phrases or even just one word, but I know it's real. I found my strength from his memory. Something you, Everett, told me to do." Turning my head to Dean, I continue, "And Dean, if you hadn't followed me immediately after the simulation, I'd still be lost. A zombie with no feelings, no emotions, a blank slate moving on autopilot."

Finally, I turned my gaze to Arno. "And Arno, if you weren't the voice of reason and the person to tell me to stop feeling sorry for myself, I definitely wouldn't be as mentally strong as I am now. What I'm saying is, I can't succeed without you guys. I need you all. I want you all to be the ones to train me, to help me become someone stronger than the damaged, destroyed little girl that left Florida all those years ago." I take a few deep breaths, my hands starting to shake as I look down at them. "I believe I was led down this road for a reason. There's no way our paths crossed by mere accident. I may not know what that reason is at the moment, but I know it's not to remain the same person I was that day at the café." I'm still looking down at my hands when I hear Everett rise from the sofa. He comes to stand in front of me, and I lift my head to meet his gaze. The expression that flashes across his face is conflicted. He doesn't want to continue with training, that's evident, but then his eyes soften. As he takes a deep breath, he cups my face in his hands, his touch instantly warming my cheeks as his emerald eyes peer into mine.

"Sloan, I'd never stop you from doing something you truly desire, but please think long and hard about your decision to continue. It will only get worse from here. Watching you today—" He stops and closes his eyes as if he's been thrown back into the observation room watching the torture play out. His jaw tenses at the mention of today. "It's hard to see you go through that, love."

I lift my hands and place them on top of his, his eyes open, revealing the pain of seeing me in such a state. "No one said this was going to be easy, right?" I whisper to him. I pull away from his hold and kiss his palm, my lips lingering for a long moment. When I look into his eyes again, I can see the internal battle within. Stop training or continue? I can't imagine the position they are in, watching me day after day fall back into the torturous ways of my childhood. I know if I were them, I'd feel the same way.

When the one you love is feeling excruciating pain that can be stopped at any moment, of course you would hit that off button and end their torture. But would you do it if that person you love asked you not to hit that button? They asked to remain in a constant state of pain, filled with mental and physical abuse, unlike anything you've ever seen. Would you listen? Would you respect their wishes, or save them from themselves?

"Everything I will experience in the simulations are all things I've already felt. Experiences I've already lived through, so going through them again is my way of rewriting my story. Rewriting the tale of the weak and timid little girl into a true heroine of her own story," I whisper, still holding his hands to my cheeks. The visible tension Everett was holding in his shoulders seems to melt away with my words. I watch the shallow rise and fall of his chest as his breathing regulates. Finally, he rests his forehead on mine.

"If you wish, love," he says to me before planting a soft kiss to the tip of my nose. Everett's strong arms wrap around me and pull me into his chest. It's more than a hug, more than an embrace. At this moment, Everett is speaking so loudly without having to say a word. He's scared—scared for my safety, for my well-being, but also scared for my mind and the state it will be in after this training comes to an end. This form of training, or torture, if you will, is what I imagine military recruits go through, or CIA operatives. The strain and torment we are forced to go through in order to be considered a Shadow is overwhelming. It's trying mentally and physically. To be brought to your absolute lowest self to see if you are able to crawl out of the hole they put you in is the real test. To remain focused, calm, and unaffected when the world around us is imploding. This is the real test.

Everett was right when he said the most difficult part of this whole training was the mental aspect. Even though it's already proven to break me, I won't let it happen twice. I'm sure of that.

CHAPTER 17

SLOAN

October 25, 2021

I've been able to dig deeper into her past. Her father and mother, if you'd even call them that, are the lowest of the low. It's a miracle she survived and escaped when she did. She's strong and the will to live is overpowering all her trauma. I admire her for that. Discovering who she is and where she comes from is only a sliver of what we need to put the pieces together and unmask the culprit behind the attacks on her. We also need to know why the job was placed on her in the first place. With the little information I have gathered about this girl, it's a mystery to me why her life is in so much danger. She's never hurt anyone, never stolen, never mingled with the wrong crowd, yet there are still powerful people out there who want to take her last breath from her lungs. Why? I've taken on more jobs within the sex trafficking organization in hopes of gath-

ering more intel on why she was initially sent to Stone Fortress. That's where I'll start.

Following my first bout with the simulation, I was able to convince Everett and the guys to allow me to move forward with training. It's still early in the day and following lunch, I will be heading back into the simulation room. If I'm not able to control every aspect of this memory, I will fail and won't be able to move on to my final test. The forty-two-hour test where I'm given a target to locate, eliminate, and escape without being harmed. Sounds easy enough.

The four of us are finishing our lunch in the lounge room when Jei and Stefan enter and motion for Everett and Dean to follow them. With their behavior during my last simulation, their privileges for viewing have been revoked, therefore, they must remain in a separate room where they'll wait for my completion. Naturally, they are furious, but they understand this is protocol and don't want to ruin any chances I have of passing this test. Before they're made to leave, they both give me a kiss and remind me to focus on my memory. This memory being Colson. Dean also reminds me not to lose the switch in my head, to always keep it in my sights, and never fully take my eyes off it.

I assure them both that I'm ready, and I watch my men leave me as the feeling of butterflies starts rumbling in my gut. I'm staring at the door, a feeling of uncertainty flooding my system. Will I be okay?

"You can do this, little one. There's no need to be

nervous now. You've already proven you can beat this," Arno says between bites of his sandwich, bringing my attention to him. Arno's dark eyes are focused on something that's not in the room. He's chewing, but I can tell he's thinking about something far off from where we are now. I let the silence between us grow as I replay his words over in my head.

"My final simulation was the hardest thing I ever had to witness for the second time in my life. Every simulation is a memory we've already experienced, but my specific memory was so mind-crushing, that I hid it from myself for so long that I forgot about it altogether. Until that day." Arno takes the last bite of his food and brushes his hands together, removing the crumbs. He leans back in his chair, tilting his head up slightly as he inhales a deep breath.

"When I was nine years old, my father made some bad business deals with the cartel. My father was a foolish man and blinded by greed and money. That was his first mistake. His second mistake was letting it slip that he had kids. This was their fuel that would spark the fire." He pauses a moment, collecting his thoughts before continuing. "My younger sisters, Emilia and Layla, five-year-old twins at the time, were the unfortunate ones."

I can't help the tears that've started to form in my eyes at the mention of his sisters. Sisters, I never knew he had. Closing his eyes, he speaks again.

"When my father couldn't pay up, the cartel sent a

few visitors to our home in Naples. The three of us were playing in the street in front of our house when our father told us to come inside. We obeyed, and once the three of us were inside, two men grabbed my sisters. I started to scream and fight, trying to loosen the men's grip on my sisters, but I was so small. My father did nothing. Fucking nothing." Arno's voice cracks, but he manages to inhale a sharp breath and regain his composure. "I was eventually restrained and tied to a chair with tape over my mouth. My father was sitting at our dining room table with a gun to the back of his head in case he decided to fight. He was a coward and never even tried in the slightest to save my sisters. I tried everything I could to loosen the rope on my arms and legs and eventually tipped the chair over. The men were telling my father the price he had to pay if he wanted all this to stop. He didn't have a dime to his name at that point. Just like that, two gunshots pierced the air, and my sisters were gone."

A sob escapes my throat as I stare at Arno's face. His eyes are still closed, head tilted back as if he's reliving that moment.

"Arno, I—I am so sorry," I manage to say, my voice cracking with sadness. He shakes his head as if there's no need to apologize.

"When my father didn't show even the slightest bit of emotion when their bodies hit the floor, the men were so revolted by his lack of empathy towards his own children that they decided to kill him too. They knew they would never see the money he owed, so why not kill the low-life piece of shit, anyway? Before they left, they came up to me and told me, 'This is what happens when you don't pay up.' My mother came home shortly after and found hell in her dining room. She couldn't handle the grief of losing her girls, three months later, she died in her sleep. She stopped taking care of herself, and I truly believe she died of a broken heart."

My hand is over my mouth and the tears have yet to subside as Arno finally opens his eyes and looks at me. He gives me a sympathetic half-smile before reaching over and wiping away the tears that have collected on my jawline.

"Don't cry for me, Sloan, I remembered their faces. They received a death far, far worse than my sisters. I made sure of that. I'm telling you this because this last simulation is going to be so fucking hard. The technology within the room is able to analyze every thought, every memory, and every traumatic event that's ever happened to you. It's going to pick the moment that affected you the most and make you relive it in perfect detail. Don't let it win. You have to stay focused and know that you've already survived that moment. Don't let it break you. You're so fucking strong, little one. I know you can do this. Now, go and prove it to everyone else."

My face is leaning into Arno's palm, my hand resting over his as he wipes away the last of my tears. The door swings open again, and Stefan is there instructing me that it's time to go. I turn to face the door and give him one nod as I slowly stand. Arno follows suit but grabs my hand before I walk towards the door. Pulling me into a tight embrace, he whispers in my ear,

"If my sisters were alive today, I imagine they'd be like you. Strong, stubborn, and fierce in every way imaginable. Now go get 'em, tiger." I squeeze him a little harder before I finally let him go, giving him one last glance and turning to follow Stefan to the simulation room again for the second time today.

Fuck, what've I gotten myself into?

CHAPTER 18

SLOAN

November 15, 2021

I have a strange suspicion that someone within the organization is behind setting up the job to kidnap Sloan, but I have yet to find proof that this is factual. I've been racking my brain trying to determine how anyone else would be able to infiltrate our highly protected system and successfully set up the job for her. The only logical explanation would be someone who has experience in the network —a past employee or a present one. We've already visited Arno and his goons, and this proved to be a waste. Although his presence at Stone Fortress is suspicious on its own, and I will figure out why he was there. For right now he is no longer a person of interest in finding Sloan's hunters. I feel like the weeks have gone by and I have gotten no closer to finding out anything.

· · ·

As I follow Stefan down the long hallway, a feeling of dread starts pooling in my stomach.

I can do this.

You can do this, Sloan.

I'm strong.

I'm in control.

I can feel Arno's presence behind me as his heavy boots echo through the hallway. As Stefan reaches for the door, I turn around to face Arno. He's already stopped walking and the expression on his face is unreadable. His hands are in his jean pockets and his eyes flick from my face to whoever is behind me. I assume it's Stefan, since he was the only other one in the hallway.

"Remember, little one, this is going to be the worst of them all. Stay focused, stay composed, and don't fuck up. I'll see you on the other side." Before I can respond to him, a sharp prick digs into the back of my neck. My legs are the first to go numb. They buckle beneath me, and the last image I see is Arno lunging for me. He cradles my limp neck before I crash to the ground and, as I stare up at his face, he gives me a wink before everything fades to black.

Shouting, loud and deep, fills my ears before I'm able to see anything. Shouts and rushed voices fill the cold, damp air around me as I peel my eyes open. Blinking what feels like a hundred times to try to quickly regain my focus. Finally, as my eyes adjust, I see the beautiful shape of the moon above me. I'm lying in a grass field, the grass cold and wet beneath me. I sit up in a rush trying to familiarize myself with where exactly I'm at. Distant yells and shouting still invade my ears when the image of a jet has me swallowing hard.

As I try to comprehend what memory I've just been thrown into, I see the silhouettes of five, maybe six men running into the clearing from the cover of the forest. Squinting my eyes, I can see Arno carrying someone, another set of guys running in front of him also carrying limp bodies thrown over their shoulders. It hits me like a jab to the gut by Mike Tyson himself.

Colson's death.

The stinging in my eyes comes without warning. I can't stop the burning behind my eyes and the grip on my heart as the pain starts flooding my chest cavity. Fuck, I can't watch this again. I can't go through this moment. Not this one. Any other memories, please. The time my father beat me so badly I was sent to the hospital, the time my mother drugged my food paralyzing me the entire night, the time my father held me under the sink until I passed out. Why this one?

Standing from where I was lying, I run as fast as I can to the jet, just as Arno disappears through the latched door. There's blood, a lot of blood, leading from the stairs and towards the rear of the plane where I spot Arno leaning over who I know is Colson. I hesitate a moment, not wanting to feel this pain again. In a moment, I feel a rush of fog swirling in my core from my gut to my chest. The familiar feeling of my emotions trying to protect me by blocking the connection from my heart to my brain. I allow it to fill me, but not entirely. I can't give in fully; I need to remain in control.

Closing my eyes for a moment, I calm the battle inside. Taking a deep breath and focusing on anything other than this moment.

Focus, Sloan.

Don't lose control.

I snap my eyes open when the sound of a familiar voice fills my head.

"I'll meet you in the pool, baby girl." Colson's voice is fading, his whispered words grabbing my heart and ripping it from my chest. As I make my way to the back of the plane, I see Everett and Dean bleeding profusely from their wounds as the guys work fast to stop their bleeding. Both of them are badly beaten, and I hadn't noticed the extent of their wounds the last time I was on this plane. I was so focused on losing Colson; I didn't stop to see.

Everett's face is discolored, swollen, even if he was conscious at this moment, I doubt he would be able to open his eyes. Dean is lying on his stomach, the whip marks so long, so deep, and so many of them are covering every inch of his back. I can no longer identify his tattoos that once covered his skin. The threat of bile rising from my stomach has me stopping in my tracks once again.

I can do this.

This has already happened and both Everett and Dean are safe now.

The fog that was swirling in my chest has become more dense and almost impossible to cut through as the inevitable image of Colson is looming ahead. I don't want to feel this. I don't want to relive this. I open my eyes and land on Arno. His eyebrows are furrowed together, and his dark eyes are on me, not an ounce of sorrow or sympathy in his gaze. It's as if he is trying to say something without actually saying it. I study his face for a moment. Trying to decipher his expression, I take a step closer to him, but the faint sound of a whisper has me stopping in my tracks.

You've already lived this.

I'm still looking at Arno and his lips aren't moving, and when I turn around to scan the airplane nobody is looking at me or even speaking. The guys are still being bandaged up, and the attention of the others is solely focused on Everett and Dean. Who said that?

Arno's brows pinch harder together as I take another step closer. I peer down over Arno's shoulder and if my heart could break all over again, the look of Colson's lifeless body just did it. His skin is so ashen gray, his eyes are shut as if he's sleeping, and the blood—there's so much blood.

You know when you're in a dream and you finally realize everything around you isn't real, so you close your eyes super tight, and when you open them again you're back in your bed safe and away from the horrors of your subconscious? Even when I close my eyes and reopen them, I'm still standing in the same spot. My legs tremble as my eyes are fixated on his beaten and bloodied body. My eyes are swelling with tears, my head is pounding with all the chaos around me, my chest is heaving, and suddenly I hear him again.

Focus on me.

I'm still staring down at Colson, who is not moving, not talking, not breathing, but I know it's him talking in my head. I know he is here, and I'll be damned if I fail this and never get the chance to avenge him.

What am I supposed to do? How do I defeat this memory? Do I allow the tears to fall? Do I just stay put and build the wall around me so I can't express the emotions that are quite literally shredding me apart on the inside? I don't understand, why is this memory a test for me? The horrors have already taken place. I can't change or alter anything. I can't go back and kill Cara. I'm just stuck. Utterly stuck in this tragic memory of watching someone I love die in front of me.

I'm beginning to feel frantic, as if time is running out and I'm moments away from failing when suddenly, something catches my eye on Colson's hip bone. A tattoo of a songbird that was once sprawled out across his lower abdomen is now sitting perched on a small branch; his wings no longer spread wide but tucked close to its body. I kneel beside him and wipe away the blood that's caked on his skin. Examining the tattoo, I look at Arno with so much confusion as he stares down at me, not understanding what I'm doing.

"What is it, Sloan?" he says to me in his deep voice. Quickly, I examine the rest of his body, wiping blood as I go, trying to review all the tattoos I know he has. The star constellation that peppered his left forearm used to have exactly twelve small stars, each one different in size. However, looking at Colson's arm now, there are only ten stars.

"This isn't possible," I say to myself as I frantically continue across his body. Colson has a scar behind his left ear. It's in the shape of a fishhook, almost. He told me he received it on one of his jobs that went wrong. While trying to escape, he was sent through a glass window that left him with a deep gash behind his ear, thus scarring into this very specific shape. I turn his limp body to the side and when I pull back his ear, there is no scar. The skin is smooth and untouched. I then grab his face and pry his mouth open, expecting to see a tongue ring present, but again there's nothing. No ring, no evidence that a ring was ever there.

What the fuck is going on?

I think of one last thing, as I place two of my fingers down on the sparrow tattoo over Colson's hip and press down. When I drag my finger along the skin, black ink follows, smearing across his skin and ruining the artwork. I stand in an instant, my eyes looking behind me to Everett and Dean, but the two of them are still unconscious. Then I turn to Arno in a hurry, grabbing him by the shoulders as I get in his face.

"This isn't Colson!" My screams echo through the air as if I'm screaming the words over and over and over again.

"This isn't Colson!"

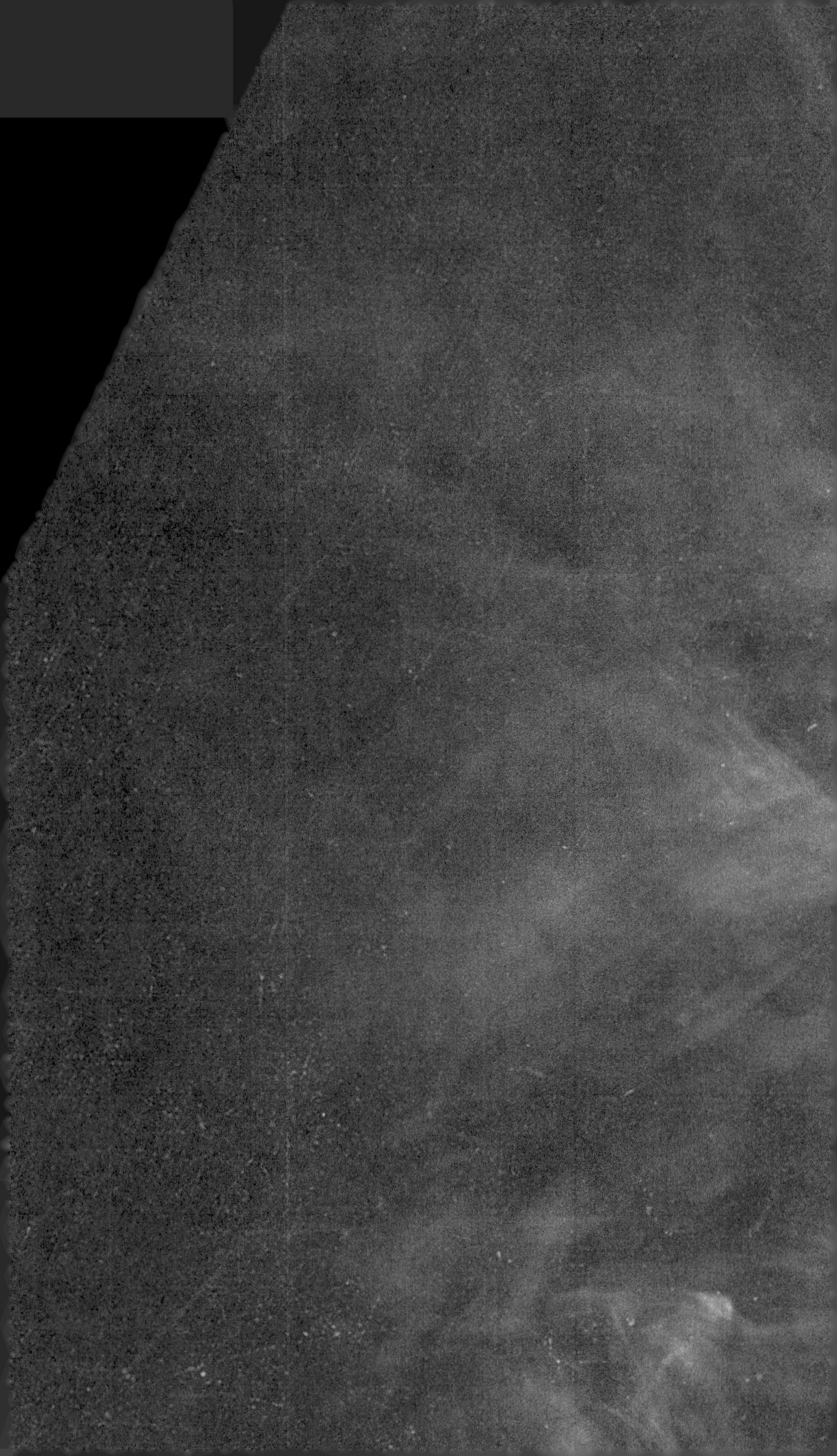

CHAPTER 19

SLOAN

A bright white light shines through the room, causing me to close my eyes as the realization of this moment hits me like a Louisville Slugger to the back of my head. My breathing is ragged and I'm trying desperately to blink the blindness away.

"Sloan, Sloan, look at me, open your eyes!" a faint voice bellows to me as I try to obey their commands.

When the silhouette of a man appears in front of me, I burst out to whomever it is, "It wasn't Colson!"

When I finally get my vision back, Arno is standing in front of me. His face contorted in confusion as he holds me still in his hands.

"Sloan, what are you talking about? It was just a memory," he says to me, his voice soft and sympathetic. He must think I'm absolutely crazy and in such denial that I'm spitting out this nonsense, but I continue to try to explain frantically. I push away his hands and stiffen my spine as I look up at him, my heart racing and thoughts of Colson still being alive flooding my brain.

"That wasn't Colson on the plane. I didn't notice it before, but his tattoos weren't real, they were all wrong, and he didn't have a tongue ring and his scar —it wasn't there, it was gone!" My words are flying out of my mouth when Everett and Dean burst through the simulation room door. I take in another deep breath as I eye them both.

"What the fuck was that?" Dean shouts, both of their gazes bouncing from Arno to me. I move past Arno, my hands now shaking as I try to explain what I saw in the simulation.

"It wasn't Colson on the plane. It must've been someone else. His tattoos were fake, all of them, and he didn't have a tongue ring. All the ink wiped away with my fingers. It's not him." I'm pleading with the guys to believe me; I need someone to believe me. Colson could still be out there.

"Listen, little one, you were in a simulation, a memory, a dream. The technology can't get it right all the time. Tattoos, facial features, and tongue rings can all be distorted. The machines go off your memory, so if you remembered something wrong, it would take that into consideration." Arno's voice is low and full of sadness as he speaks behind me. I'm still looking at Dean and Everett as I silently beg them to believe me.

"What if I'm right, though? What if whoever's in the grave is not Colson and he's still out there?" The room is so silent, so painfully silent, I can hear my own heart banging in my chest. "Please, you have to believe me. I know all of Colson's tattoos by heart. I would always trace them with my finger when we fell asleep together. He loved the feeling." I hold back my sob. "I can tell you every tattoo he has, where it's at, and what it looks like. I promise."

"Arno, can the simulation be wrong? Can it interpret a memory and fill in the blanks with what it thinks is right?" Everett asks in a stern voice, his eyebrows pinched so hard together that the creases in his forehead appear.

"No, it's designed to only project what the memory is, such as what Sloan remembers or saw. It can't input information such as a fake tattoo just to piece the memory together," Arno replies. Sweat is beading across my hairline now; my insides are rattling, and my fingers are going numb. I sense as though I may have a panic attack with this new realization.

"So, you're saying, if Sloan says she saw fake tattoos, or no scars, or no piercing, that's exactly what she saw that day?" Dean asks as we all stare at Arno for his response.

"Yes, if she said that's what she saw in the simulation, that's what she would have seen that day. The mind sometimes sees things but doesn't comprehend them right away. A situation can be so traumatic that the brain doesn't have the capacity to register everything at once. Our minds keep things in our subconscious until triggered again, such as this simulation of the event."

Bile rises up in my throat and my legs feel as though I'm about to fall. Colson could still be alive. "How do we know this for sure?" Everett says in a low hoarse voice, anger slowly rising as the vein in his neck grows thicker. Arno is staring at Everett, the answer on his tongue but not wanting to say it.

"Fuck, mate, spit it out!" Dean's voice startles me, making me jump at his side. Arno inhales a deep breath, his eyes closing as he rubs down his face with his hands.

"Fuckkkk, we'd have to dig up the grave to verify."

The room goes black, and I've completely lost all function of my legs as my panic attack takes over, and I lose consciousness right then and there.

———

I awaken to the sound of several voices bouncing back and forth from either side of me. Everything sounds so far away, like I'm in a long, narrow tunnel. Peeling open my eyes, I see the outline of a man sitting at my feet. I lift my hand to rub my face and notice I'm lying on a plush sofa.

Colson.

Sitting straight up, I see it's Dean sitting at my feet, his face suddenly turning to face me as I quickly spring forward.

"Whoa, easy, baby girl. Are you alright? You hit your head when you passed out," Dean asks as he positions himself to the side of me, so I don't roll off the sofa. I rub my eyes with the palms of my hands and hear someone arguing behind me. Turning my head, I see Everett talking with someone I've never seen before.

"You're telling me you didn't check his identification tag before you put him in the fucking ground?" Everett bellows at the man who looks just as frustrated as Everett. He's an older man, maybe in his mid-fifties, and he's wearing black slacks and a long-sleeved, white button-up shirt. As Everett questions him, his hands are out in front of him in a surrender-type gesture, as if to try to calm Everett down.

"The tags are in place to identify those we can't identify visually. It looked just like Colson, we figured we didn't need to check the tag," the man says to Everett, but my attention is suddenly on Arno who appears from beside Everett in a fury.

"That's your fucking job!" Arno's tone is murderous as he raises his hands in the air before stomping away. The end of the sofa is jostled as Dean stands up and makes his way over to the man everyone is currently yelling at.

"It's been six months—six fucking months! No telling what they're doing to him, that is, if he's even still alive at this point." Dean is in the man's face now, and I half expect him to end the man's life right here in the lounge room. Everett places his hand on Dean's shoulder before speaking again.

"Go do what you have to do. You'll inform us immediately either way if it's Colson or if it isn't. Understood?" The man nods once to Everett and then turns to leave, not saying another word. I swing my legs over the sofa and rest my head in my hands. Six months. It's been six months since we left Ireland. Could he really be alive? Why switch him out with a decoy? What could they possibly need with Colson?

"What have we done?" I whisper in my hands, the feeling of guilt pooling in my stomach as I try not to imagine Colson and what he could possibly be going through at this exact moment. The room is quiet except for the footsteps of Dean, who is pacing the length of the small room as we all wait for the confirmation.

In my head, I play back the simulation step by step, visualizing everything I saw and everything I missed that day on the plane. His tattoos for certain were not his tattoos. The scar behind his ear, and his tongue ring—everything was different. But his face...he looked just like Colson. He looked so much like Colson that everyone that day believed it to be him, Arno, Stefan, Jei, and me. Everett and Dean were unconscious, so they weren't able to identify him, but how could he have fooled so many of us?

Minutes turn into hours and my stomach is in such a knot I can hardly stand. Arno left about a half hour ago to rewatch my simulation to try to pinpoint anything we may have missed. Dean and Everett are huddled around their laptop to watch the camera footage from the body cams The Shadows were wearing that day as well. And me, well I'm still sitting on the couch, my hands shaking as I wait for the door to open and someone to tell me that Colson is in fact not the person laying six feet underground.

"We've watched this clip five times already, mate, there's nothing there." I hear Dean say to Everett as he rewinds the same clip again.

"There's always something, we just have to find it," Everett retorts as he hits play on the clip for the sixth time. It's a clip of Cara talking with the three of them as they all take blow after blow after blow. The sound of the whip hitting Dean makes my stomach twist, and I can't take it any longer. Standing from the sofa, I make my way out of the room.

I don't know where I'm going. I decide to walk the hallway, anywhere, is better than listening to my guys being tortured because of me. Before I reach the end of the hallway, I hear Everett's voice behind me.

"We've found something, love." I turn to face him, his hands in his pants pockets, but his expression is unreadable. He's calm, but the way his eyes are narrowed slightly shows he is trying to hide his true emotions. He waits for me to reach him as I make my way back down the hallway. Stopping in front of him, I crane my neck up towards his and wait. Pulling a hand out from his pocket, he wraps it around my lower back and pulls me flush to his chest. His other hand cradles my neck, and he kisses my lips so softly, so gently, that I lose myself for a moment.

I kiss him back. The stress and tension I was holding onto slowly begins to melt away, like a candle dripping its hot wax. His hand squeezes my hip as our kiss deepens. I can think of a million other things we need to do right now, but at this moment, we both need this. A moment where nothing else matters, where there is no stress, no anxiety, just a moment of peace.

I lean into Everett harder, needing him more than I realized. I snake my hands up his shirt and glide them across his chest. He flexes his abdomen against my touch, making all the crevices and grooves of his muscles poke out. I'm suddenly spun around, my back flush to the wall as Everett presses his body against mine, the bulge in his pants showing me how much he truly needs this. The click of the door snaps me out of my paradise with Everett as Dean steps into the hallway.

"Sorry, love, but you're going to need to see this," Dean says to the both of us. I rest my forehead on Everett's chest for a moment, soaking in his touch and allowing him to fully calm my nerves before I reluctantly peel myself away from him. Dean sits at the table with the laptop and pulls out a chair to sit beside him. Everett follows suit and takes a seat on my other side. Dean faces the laptop screen towards me, the mouse hovering over the play button.

"Now, it's fast, but watch the trapdoor to the far

right of the screen right before the camera goes out." I nod my understanding as Dean hits the play button. I focus all my attention on the corner of the screen. The picture is wobbly as the Shadow member fumbles with the camera that's pinched between two stones of the wall and the building the guys were held in. Just as the gunshot pierces the air in the room, the camera jerks to the side, and I catch a glimpse of the trapdoor.

"You see it?" Everett says from my side, but I'm confused.

"No. All I saw was the trapdoor. What am I missing?"

"Here, I'll play it again frame by frame," Dean says to me, turning the laptop towards him a bit to control the settings. The picture moves in slow motion, frame by frame, until the trapdoor comes into view once again. As the frame stops, I can make out the image of a man's face hiding beneath the door. The next frame comes, and the door opens more, allowing me to see the profile of a man who looks familiar. My jaw opens wide as I turn to face Everett.

"Is that—?" I don't have to say his name. Everett is already nodding his answer as I take in a sharp gasp.

"Callum?"

CHAPTER 20

SLOAN

January 12, 2022

What the fuck is happening? My mind can't keep up with the nonsense we've experienced these past few months. Since getting the job to kidnap Sloan, everything has been complete and utter chaos. We have never been so confused and uncertain about something as we all are now. Dean and Sloan were taken, and fuck, Dean almost died. Who is doing this and why?! I'm starting to lose my patience, and I know Everett and Dean are as well. We don't know what to do. We know we have to find Van and torture and kill the fuck out of him for what he did in the warehouse, but we need to understand why he did it in the first place. There are too many unanswered questions, and I'm not sure how to get the answers. I have another job coming up, and I have a strong suspicion I'll be able to get a few answers then.

. . .

I haven't said a word since seeing Callum on the video. I truly have no words. Everett's twin brother, his fucking brother, is behind all this shit somehow. But why? Everett is his brother, and to allow the torture of him and his closest friends under his watch is one of the purest forms of evil. I'm staring at Callum's profile—the sounds of Everett and Dean conversing behind me are muffled by the chaos swirling in my head. It's not until Dean raises his voice in the realization of something that I turn my head from the laptop to see what they are talking about.

"It was him, mate! It was fucking Cal who put the job up for Sloan! He is the only other person that could have infiltrated the system without being detected. You and I both know he is proficient at hacking and computers. It has to be him." Dean's speaking so fast it's hard for me to keep up. I look between both of them, realizing it does make sense. He would have the knowledge to do such a thing, but the question still stands as to why?

Everett brushes his hand through his hair, frustration etched across his face. I never had siblings growing up, so I can't even begin to imagine the betrayal he must feel knowing his brother was a part of the most brutal torture he's ever gone through. The hurt and pain of knowing your own blood wanted to inflict excruciating pain without a single bit of remorse is heart-wrenching. I don't know how close they were growing up, but I can imagine being a twin would create a bond that no other siblings would understand. They share the same DNA. They look identical. They are one and the same. As much as Everett claims he has no connection or relationship with his brother, I have a feeling deep down this whole situation hurts in a way that is unique to him.

I stand from where I'm sitting at the table and make my way over to where Everett's standing. Before I can wrap my arms around him and try to ease the hurricane that is building within him, the door opens in a whirl. Arno stands in the doorway with dirt and mud caked to his hands and extending up his arms. Sweat is trailing down his face as he tries to catch his breath. The three of us stare at him anxiously waiting for him to speak and explain why he's in such a state. He doesn't get the chance before the man who is responsible for identifying the deceased members of the organization trails in behind him.

He is equally dirty, but his demeanor is calmer as he runs a white cloth through his hands, removing the dirt that was once there. Moving past Arno, he makes his way into the lounge, his head hanging low as he continues with the now dirt-covered cloth.

"I'm not sure if this news will be considered good or bad," the man starts, his head still hanging low before he takes a deep breath. Lifting his head, he exposes the pained look in his eyes. "The man who is currently buried outside is, in fact, not Colson Cain." The room is silent, I swear I can hear my own blood flowing in my veins. As if this has all been a bad dream, my mind whirls with the hope that Colson could still be alive.

Dean lunges for the man, grips his collar, and hoists him up, slamming him to the wall. No one has enough time to react. The fury that has been unleashed is the darkness that resides deep inside Dean.

"Six fucking months! We could've been searching for him! Six fucking months!" Dean's voice travels throughout the small room, pure rage coursing through his body. Just as he lifts his fist in the air, Everett grabs Dean from behind, trying to pull him away from the man's face. As quick as Everett is, Dean's sheer strength is at a new level after hearing this news. Dean's knuckles make contact with the man's nose. The audible crunch of bones cracking splinters the air, and I wince at the sound. Blood pours from his nose as he grabs his face with both hands, backing away to the door and disappearing down the hall.

"Dean! Dean, relax, mate! We need to pull it together if we're going to find Colson!" Everett bellows at Dean, getting in his face and trying to pull Dean out of his state of rage. I pinch my eyes shut and take a few deep breaths as the realization of Colson possibly being alive fills my soul even more. A hand gently lands on my shoulder, giving me a small squeeze as I open my eyes to Arno standing beside me.

"How could I have been so stupid?" he whispers to me, his head lowers toward the ground, pain evident across his face. "I should have known; I should have seen the signs. I should've checked his identification myself. This is my fault too, Sloan. I'm so sorry." I turn to face him, his hand falling away from my shoulder.

"Look at me, Arno. If this is your fault, then it's my fault too. I did exactly what you told me not to do. I let my emotions take hold of me and because of that, I missed all the signs. We can make it up to him and find him, save him, and bring him home." His dark eyes meet mine; his brows pinch together, causing small creases to form on his forehead. He gives me a slight nod before lifting his head to Everett and Dean, where Everett is still trying to calm Dean down.

"Hey, you two, shut the fuck up, and let's get to finding Colson! Arguing and complaining about our mistakes won't get us any closer to finding him. Pull yourselves together, and let's get to work." The smile that creeps across my face at Arno's words fills me with the hope that Colson could very well be alive.

Colson, alive.

I turn myself around, facing my guys as they slowly bring themselves down from their justifiable fit of rage. Looking at Dean, I can visibly see the tension ease from his shoulders as Everett rights his shirt from where Dean was clutching it. I step closer to the two of them, giving them both a sympathetic look.

"What do we know? We know the location of their compound. We know they have an underground tunnel system that allows them to move around undetected. We know who has him, we know another player in their game, and we know they still have Colson. My thoughts are he's still on the compound somewhere, just not in the same holding room as you were in last time. They don't know that we know they have a tunnel system. We need to infiltrate their underground network and determine where they could be holding him and why." As I speak, I look between all three of them. Their expressions are pensive as they take in all the information I've listed. With a nod, Dean takes a step towards me. His steel-gray eyes are sharp as he stares deep into my eyes.

"You're right, baby girl. You're absolutely fucking right." He cups my cheek with his hand and gently brushes his thumb across my skin. After a moment, he drops his hand and turns to Everett.

"We also know that Cal is definitely involved now. Which leads me to believe that his ties with the Irish mob are deeper than we initially thought." The sound of keys on the laptop has me turning to see Arno. He's sitting at the table, his large frame hunched over as his fingers type away a mile a minute.

"Before we arrived at the compound, we had surveillance being run from our team. Maybe I missed something on the footage we collected from the outside of the building that could tell us more about their blueprints of the compound," Arno says to the room, not looking up from the computer screen as his fingers continue clicking away at the keys. Dean takes up the seat beside him, and before I grab a seat myself, I turn to see Everett, his far-away gaze causing me to stop.

"What is it?" I say to him, making my way over to where he stands. He doesn't answer me right away, instead his eyes seem to be glossed over. His thoughts take him somewhere other than this room. He seems as if he's holding his breath, and when I place my hand on his chest, he flinches, his eyes snapping down to me.

"Are you okay?" I whisper, his chest finally rising with a deep inhale of a breath. "What are you thinking about?"

He places his hand over mine that's still resting on his chest.

"What if we were all supposed to be switched with decoys? What if that was the plan all along, but you all got to us before they could finish swapping us out? What if they knew you all were coming—they anticipated the rescue and planned for it?" I tilt my head at his theory. It makes sense, but it still doesn't answer the question, why?

"It's possible, but why go to such great lengths to find decoys that look identical to you three? What's the purpose of that?" The sound of typing stops as Dean and Arno listen to Everett's theory. No one speaks. The silence grows deafening as the four of us try to find an answer to this question. I start pacing the room, my mind racing with possible answers, but none really feel accurate. Why switch my guys out? What is the possible gain for Cara by doing such an extreme act? Colson. Dean. Everett. What did Cara want in the first place? What is her end game?

Me.

I stop moving. My heart picks up speed as realization dawns on me. The whole reason for the meeting in the first place was to learn my whereabouts. She wants me. She wants to eliminate me, so she and Cormick are the only two others who will inherit the Wallace family fortune. She will then become the leader, the head of the mob itself. She knew after taking my guys, there would be repercussions, so she had a plan already in place for when that happened. However, we were too quick for her plan to be completed. She was only able to successfully swap Colson for his decoy, but if she had the right amount of time, she would have done so with Dean and Everett as well.

I clap my hands together, causing the guys to turn their attention to me. Whirling around, I can't help the smile that starts forming on my face.

"I know why she wanted to swap out the three of you for decoys!" My voice travels through the room, my voice almost a shout as excitement bubbles in my chest. "What does Cara ultimately want? What does she have that would allow her to get close to me without being in my presence herself?" I pause, allowing the guys to catch up with my train of thought. "What would be the benefit of her swapping you three out and allowing us to rescue who we would have thought was the real you? You see, it makes sense!" I run over to the table and stand on the opposite side, allowing me to see each of their faces as I continue to explain. "If she was able to swap Dean and Colson out with look-alikes, she would also be able to switch Everett with Callum!" Dean and Everett instantly look at each other, their eyes growing as round as saucers.

"Wait, Callum? As in your twin brother, Callum?" Arno is shaking his head in confusion, and I quickly realize he hasn't seen the footage of Callum in the trap door yet. I quickly grab the laptop, spin it around, and load the video where the guys discovered Callum hiding beneath the coverage of the door.

"What the fuck, mate? Your brother is linked in with Cara and the Irish mob? You know what this means, don't you?" Arno asks the table, now making me a little confused as to what he means. I shake my head, as do Dean and Everett. "If your brother Cal is with Cara, as in together with Cara, he will be inheriting a position in the mob with Cara. That could have been his plan all along. Seduce Cara and trick her into thinking he loves her, only to inherit the Wallace family fortune once all the other players have been eliminated."

I rub my temple with my hands as an intense headache builds inside my skull. What the actual fuck. If this theory is right, then this whole situation

I'm currently in is all because of power, money, and status. Money will make people do some crazy shit, but this plan is so intense and so elaborate that it's truly hard to believe. Callum had all his chest pieces in a row and played his game, always three moves ahead of us.

"It's plausible, yes. This all just seems so above Cal with so many moving parts and details that it's crazy to think that he constructed this elaborate plan. From setting the job up for Sloan, sending her to Stone Fortress—which is still confusing to me—to sending her to the warehouse." Everett pauses, his head lifting a bit higher from the table as his eyes dart from Dean and me. "What about Van?" I can't help my mouth falling open at the sound of Van's name. To be honest, I'd forgotten about him until now. Why is he connected? I let out a long sigh as I get to my feet and start pacing the room once again.

"This is all so confusing," I mutter, mainly to myself, but Dean responds with an agreeable huff. He stands and makes his way to the fridge, retrieving four water bottles and placing them on the table. I grab mine, twisting the top and chugging half of the ice-cold water.

"We know Van is connected to Stone Fortress. What if he was merely a pawn in the grand scheme of things? Van isn't the smartest of the bunch—we know that. Maybe it's simpler than we think. Callum meant to be there that night you were being auctioned off. What if Van was the middleman to get to Sloan? Van could have been the man to unlock the door to the auction where Callum would have had the chance to get Sloan in a way that seemed legitimate," Dean says to us all, his lip curling in a snarl at the mention of Van. If we ever find that man, I can't even imagine the death that Dean has planned for him.

I take a seat at the table and place the almost-empty water bottle in front of me as I watch a drop of condensation start trailing down the side of the plastic. Closing my eyes, I try to remember the last time I saw Colson, the real Colson, alive. What he said to me before leaving the castle and heading to the meeting in Ireland. He promised he would come back; he promised me. Today seems as if it's been the longest day of my life. The simulation, Colson not being dead in his grave, Callum and his cruel intentions. Everything comes flowing in on me at once.

My chest starts to ache as if my sternum is closing in on me, causing my ribs to splinter within. *Where are you, Colson? What have they been doing to you this whole time?*

"He must think we've forgotten about him." A sob escapes my throat as a lone tear falls from my eye. "Six months. He's been somewhere for six months. God only knows what they've been doing to him just to learn my location." I can't open my eyes. Images of his beautiful hazel eyes, long blond hair, and golden skin skate through my vision.

In a moment, my quiet sob turns into a full-blown hysterical fit of crying. Standing from the table, I cover my face with my hands and quickly make my way out of the room. Running down the hall, I burst through the women's locker room doors, still holding my now tear-soaked face. I don't know why, but I find myself standing in my favorite shower stall and turning the water on to a freezing temperature. Standing under the ice-cold spray, I tilt my head to the ceiling and let the icy water pepper my face. I'm still fully clothed when I feel that unmistakable feeling of someone watching me. I know it's him. His presence feels different from everyone else's.

My skin turns hot even though I'm standing beneath ice-cold water. Butterflies erupt in my belly, and my heart races just from his eyes being on me. It's a feeling that no one else can create within me but him.

"Everett, please, I need a moment," I say into the spray, water bouncing off my lips as I speak. He doesn't respond to me, but he also doesn't leave. Truthfully, I don't want him to leave, but I also hate crying in front of anybody. Hoping he finds a bench and waits for me to regain my composure, I turn away from the glass door of the shower and face the tiled wall, allowing myself to cry the tears I've been trying so hard to hold in. Lowering my head, I let myself feel, let the tsunami of pain and guilt flow into every crease and crevice of my body. I need to let myself feel everything. I need to allow the pain to hurt, bruise, and beat me from within. I desperately need to feel everything so I can release this box of darkness and focus all my energy on finding Colson.

I don't hear the glass door open, but when Everett wraps his arms around my body, I no longer feel out of control. Slowly, my body begins to relax, and his warm embrace wraps tightly around my body. The feeling of stillness slowly takes over. My once raging wildfire of hurt and anguish now feels like a thunderous rainstorm reaching an end.

"Colson will never give up, nor will he surrender. He is trained for situations like these. He's strong. He will survive this. We're going to find him."

CHAPTER 21

SLOAN

February 1, 2022

The job was a shit show, an absolute fucking shit show. This specific job has sat with me more so than others due to the fact that the victims are so young—too young. I was sent to kill multiple targets in a warehouse where our intel informed us there were several females being kept in cages. They would have ultimately been sent off to be sold, but this warehouse was their holding compound, so to speak. It was awful. So many girls, barely teenagers and some so much younger, were kept like animals in metal cages where they could hardly move. We are not, under any circumstance, allowed to converse with the victims we save. However, I was specifically drawn to one girl in particular. She was unnervingly calm. Her composure and maturity with the whole situation she was currently in had my curiosity heightened. When the girls were brought to the safe location where *they were given more clothes, food, and water, and I could confront her. She informed me that her name was Willow, a twenty-one-year-old from the UK. When I asked how she was so calm, she told me she knew she would be saved. She was expecting someone else to do the saving but, nevertheless she knew someone was coming to save her. Before I could ask who she thought was going to save her, I was escorted out and scolded for conversing with the victims. This small conversation I had with Willow has been on a loop in my head ever since.*

Sitting at the kitchen island, my eyes start to feel heavy as I look over the blueprints of the Wallace compound for what feels like the millionth time. Everett, Dean, Arno, and I came back to the house after I finished up in the locker room to sit and plan our next move. We decided we would go in with a small team once again, but would allow for more surveillance this time, hoping to spot Colson. Since getting home, Everett and Dean have been in the office working with the tech Shadows to try to devise a plan to get surveillance in without being detected. Arno and I have been in the kitchen learning everything we can about the compound from satellite maps, GPS coordinates, and land surveys from the past that we've been fortunate enough to find.

Taking a break from looking over the maps that are sprawled out before me, I stand up from my chair and arch my back, stretching my tight muscles and letting out a groan. I rub my eyes with the palms of my hands, rubbing so hard they begin to water.

"Why don't you turn in for the night? You've had an extremely long day. You need to get some rest," Arno says to me, as I continue rubbing my face.

"I can't. We need to keep going. Colson's been out there for far too long. I won't be able to rest until he's home safe." A yawn escapes my mouth as I make my way to the coffeepot to start a fresh pot. Before I'm even able to grab the pot, Dean's hand is over mine.

"He's right, love, you've had the longest day out of all of us. From the simulation to everything else. You need to rest."

I bow my head, knowing they are both right, but how can I rest comfortably in my bed knowing he's out there? What state is he currently in? The images of him being beaten and tortured flash through my brain and I squeeze my eyes shut, not wanting to see the horrors of what he's been through.

"Don't do that. Don't create fake scenarios in your head about what he is possibly going through. They will destroy you." Arno's tone is somber, but his words feel like he is speaking from experience. I turn to look at him. His head is down and he looks to be examining the maps still, but his eyes are in a far-off place.

"He's right, you know," Dean whispers in my ear. "Come, I'll help you to bed." Accepting that there is no arguing with these men, I interlock my fingers with Dean's and follow him to the stairs.

"Goodnight Arno," I say to him, his eyes lifting to meet mine. "Goodnight, little one," he replies to me with a small smile, pulling at his cheek.

Dean and I make our way up the stairs and straight to Colson's room. We've become so used to sleeping in his bed since he's been gone, it's almost like we gravitate here rather than our own rooms. Dean makes his way to the nightstand, flipping on the switch and illuminating the room with the warmth of the bedside lamp. He then makes his way to Colson's dresser and pulls out one of his shirts before turning back to me, where I sit on the edge of the bed.

"Tell me he's alive, Dean. Tell me he's okay," I whisper, not allowing my voice to crack as the pain starts creeping up my throat once more. Dean kneels in front of me, his hands resting on my thighs as he lowers his head to look me in the eye.

"If I know Colson, and I know I do, he really is okay. He is fighting like hell to get back to you. He loves you Sloan, he's never loved another being as much as he loves you. He wouldn't give up on you, on us, on this wild life we've created together. He's alive, baby girl, and we are going to find him." Tears form in my eyes and one starts sliding down my cheek. Dean wipes it away before it reaches my jawline and holds my face with both of his large hands.

"Don't do that. Don't cry. We need you to be strong and focused. Don't lose yourself in the thoughts you create in your head. Keep your eyes steady and know we'll get him back." I nod my head once. He's right. I need to stay focused and ready, even if that means getting some rest. Dean kisses the tip of my nose before saying, "Good girl. Now up to bed." He pulls the covers down and gestures for me to crawl under. Once I'm fully underneath the blankets, he covers me up and brushes my hair back from my head. His fingers tickle my cheek as he does.

"Stay with me until I fall asleep, please," I whisper to him. Dean doesn't answer me right away, instead he continues to brush my hair back with his fingers, scratching my scalp ever so lightly. I close my eyes at his touch, the sensation so soothing, so calming, I'm quickly drifting off to sleep before I know it.

"Colson, please, please wake up. Please don't leave me." I'm staring down at Colson's face, the life inside his eyes slowly drifting away from me. Tears are gushing from my eyes as I'm hunched over his body. This can't be happening; this can't be how our story ends. Not like this. We never even had the chance to live. I choke out a sob from my throat as I grab his shoulders and shake violently trying to wake up, but it's no use. He's gone. His body is heavy in my grasp, and his hand falls from my arm as the fight inside him ends.

"Colson! Please, Colson, don't leave me like this!" My vision blurs from the number of tears now blocking my vision. My body is shaking back and forth as I continue to cry. Someone behind me calls my name.

"Sloan, Sloan, open your eyes." I know whose voice it is, but I can't turn around to see. Still, he continues to call me. "Open your eyes, love." Colson's body is fading away—his body that was once in front of me has almost completely disappeared. The room around me is becoming brighter, as if I'm staring into a light.

"Sloan, open your eyes. You're dreaming." Everett's voice becomes clearer as I'm able to open my eyes. The plane where I was kneeling has now turned into a familiar bedroom. I'm lying on my side, Everett's body facing me as he rests on his elbow hovering over me.

"Everett?" I whisper in a sleepy voice.

"Yes, I'm here and so is Dean." I turn my head slightly and see Dean behind me snuggled to my back as his hand starts rubbing my back. I sit up straight, realizing it was all a dream. My cheeks feel tight with dried tears, and I rub down my face with my hands.

"Are you okay? You were having a nightmare," Dean says from my left, his voice sounding equally tired as mine.

"Yes, I'm fine. I'm sorry I woke you both. I didn —" Everett cuts me off before I can continue.

"You don't need to apologize to us, love. We just want to make sure you're okay." I turn my head and look over at him. Everett is still propped on his elbow as he stares at me. He's shirtless and his hair is disheveled in that sexy "I woke up like this" kind of way. The blankets are resting at his hip, and he couldn't look sexier if he tried. I give him a small smile and nod my head once.

I lay back down, curling my body into his large chest as Dean settles in behind me. He, too, is shirtless and starts peppering my back with soft kisses.

"We'll find him, baby girl. I promise," Everett whispers into my hair as he starts kissing my forehead. The three of us lay together, legs and arms circling one another, the warmth of their skin heating mine as my men continue rubbing and kissing my body. It doesn't take long until I feel the undeniable bulge of Dean's hard length pressed up against my ass. Arching my back, I press my ass harder into him, eliciting a groan from his mouth as he kisses my ear. His warm breath fanning over the sensitive spot, giving me chills.

I reach for Everett's face, desperate for more, our lips colliding as I hold on to his face. Everett presses his body into mine even harder, his length stiffening against my stomach as we continue to drink each other. His touch is bruising, as is Dean's. Their hands roam over my body, pushing my shirt up and over my head in a frenzy.

Have you ever needed a distraction so badly you morph into a completely different version of yourself to escape the world around you? I have never wanted or needed a distraction from the pain of losing Colson more than I do at this exact moment. Pulling my lips from Everett, I push his body away from mine and jump up, swinging my leg over his waist to straddle him.

My pussy is already slick with arousal as I start rubbing against his hard cock. His hands find my waist, pushing me further into him as he lets out a groan deep in his chest. Looking down at Everett, I watch as his head leans back, eyes closed and his mouth slightly open, as he savors the warmth between us. Placing my hands over his, we both move in synchronicity, both our bodies becoming one.

Peering over my shoulder, I notice Dean is no longer on the bed. I dart my head to the side, but I'm instantly stopped with a hand to my throat, my head being forced back. Looking up at the ceiling, I feel the dip of the bed behind me. Smiling to myself, I whisper in a husky voice, "Harder, Dean." A low, deep chuckle fills my ear as he rests his face against mine.

"As you wish, baby girl." Dean applies more pressure around my neck, and I moan in satisfaction. Suddenly, Everett lifts my body off his and lines his cock up with my entrance before slamming me on top of him once more, fully seating himself inside me.

"Oh, God!" I scream out. The sudden pain of him stretching me has my back arching with desire. I want more. I need more.

"'Atta girl, love, you take me so well." Everett's voice is primal as he lifts me once more and thrusts even harder this time, eliciting a gasp from me. My pussy clenches around his length, an orgasm forming deep in my core as he continues thrusting over and over again. Dean continues to hold me by my throat, but then he slides his other hand around my hip and down my abdomen. When his fingers reach my already swollen clit, I see stars.

Leaning my head back, I feel Dean's hard body against my back. His large frame also straddles Everett's lower legs as his cock presses softly against my ass.

"Oh, my God, I-I—" I'm so lost in the feel of both of them, the sound of Everett and I slapping against one another, the pleasure building rapidly between my legs, the pressure of Dean's hand tightening around my neck. When my orgasm finally crashes through me, my whole body tenses as Dean squeezes my neck just a little harder before he slowly releases me. The pleasure is already intense, but when Dean clasps his hand around my clit, applying pressure to my throbbing center, I lose all sense of sound.

I'm completely high off the feeling of both of them playing with my body in such a way I don't know where the pleasure starts and where it ends. Muffled sounds fill my head, but I can't understand who is talking or what they're saying. I never want this feeling to stop. I never want it to end. My body is suddenly lifted from where it once was, and I'm being thrown onto the bed once more. Lying face down, I feel a pair of strong hands wrap around my hips as my body is being jerked to the end of the bed.

"My turn. Now hold on, sweetheart, this may hurt

a bit," Dean growls from behind me. Before I'm fully recovered from my last orgasm, Dean's thrusting his hard cock into my pulsating pussy so hard that my head falls to the bed.

"Fuckkk, your pussy is so fucking perfect," he moans, continuing to pull out slowly and then slam back into me. The pain quickly turns into pleasure as my pussy stretches around his thick length. Clenching around him, my body is already reaching for that next orgasm as my body tightens; every muscle trembles from the euphoria that is combusting inside me.

Pressing my face firmly to the bed, I scream as Dean's thrusts become harder and more violent, as if he's letting his darkness fill the void within him. I enjoy the pain—it reminds me that I'm alive, but this side of Dean is almost dangerous. Like he forgets where he's at, who he's with, and starts seeing red as he fucks me harder and harder. My screams turn to a plea as Dean grabs my shoulders, pulling me deeper into him. The sound of our skin slapping together fills the room.

"Look at me, love." Everett's voice has me lifting my head from the bed. Everett's expression is cool as his eyes lock on mine, an understanding between us that Dean needs this release. He needs his aggression to be set free. He's been holding it in for far too long, his intensity needs to be released. Everett rests his forehead on mine, his hand sliding up my cheek and pulling my face to his. The moment our lips meet, I melt. Our lips mold together as my body continues to tense around Dean, his thrusts begin to slow as he reaches his orgasm. With one final bruising thrust, he releases inside me, a primal growl erupting from his chest as he drops his head back.

Still kissing Everett, I feel Dean's hands ease their grip from my shoulders. His cock still buried inside me, Dean slides one hand down my back and around my hip to my clit, where he starts making circular motions. I can't help the moans that slip from my mouth into Everett's, but when Dean whispers in my ear,

"You didn't think I would leave you behind, did you?" His warm breath has me shivering, and, just like that, I'm crashing through another toe-curling orgasm. I'm pressing my forehead into Everett's as he holds my head up. My whole body trembles through the pleasure as Dean's cock slowly slips from my pussy. As soon as my body is truly fucked, I collapse to the bed. Dean rises from the bed where he makes his way to Colson's bathroom, where he retrieves a warm washcloth. Climbing back on to the bed, he gently starts cleaning me up. The warmth from the cloth feeling so delicious, I let out a satisfied groan. As Dean finishes up, Everett pulls the blankets over my naked body and brushes my hair back from my face before he kisses my forehead.

"Get some sleep, baby girl." With that, I fall into a deep sleep, no strength left inside me for anymore nightmares throughout the night.

Fuck, I love my men.

CHAPTER 22

SLOAN

March 2, 2022

   We have a meeting set up with Sloan's supposed half siblings. As much as I want her to have family, this meeting and everything about it feels so wrong. Nothing involving the Irish mob is trustworthy, and I can't shake the feeling deep in my core that this may be the biggest mistake Everett, Dean, and I make as professionals. I love her—we all do—and sometimes love makes you do stupid shit. All she's ever wanted was a family that loves and cares for her, so if that means putting ourselves in danger in hopes of giving her exactly what she wants, so be it. I will come back to my girl. There is no denying that. Nobody on this earth will keep me from the one person who showed me what love actually feels like. In this life or the next, I will come back to her. She's my world now, the reason my heart beats fast when I see her smile. She's the angel the heavens have sent to this earth to stop me from falling into the *depths of the dark. No one will ever take her from me. Mark my words.*

Flipping through Colson's journal, I can't help but read her name, *Willow*. She was found in a cage with barely anything on to keep her warm. My stomach turns as I imagine seeing row after row of little girls terrified and huddled close to their bodies as they try to keep warm. Those girls were someone's child, sister, cousin, friend. Who could do such a thing? Sadly, there are many cases out there where the victims are not as lucky as those Colson saved that day. Bile is churning in my stomach, and I have to close the journal before I lose it.

Sitting here at the kitchen island alone, I think to myself. I was one of those girls. I was once locked in a room awaiting my time to be sold off to the devil's creations who would have done horrible, awful things to me. Colson saved me, too, from a fate I can't even let my mind imagine. Stone Fortress was my prison for the short time I was there. A beautiful castle that hides the horrors of what truly occurs inside behind a facade of wealth and power. It's brilliant really. No one would suspect such a gorgeous exterior to hold such an ugly secret.

I take a sip of my water and then my mind goes to Nastia and the others. They didn't make it out like I did. My eyes sting at the thought. Are they still alive? Is Nastia still alive? Just then, the front door opens and I hear Arno's deep voice call out to me as he enters the kitchen.

"One order of sweet and sour chicken smothered in extra sauce along with fried rice and two spring rolls. Anything else I can get for you, Your Majesty?" Arno chuckles at his own joke as he slides over the takeaway containers before plopping down on a bar stool and grabbing his own container. Flipping open his container, he looks over his teriyaki chicken, smiling as he licks his lips with anticipation. I don't answer him, so when the room goes silent, he looks up at me with confusion.

"You alright, little one? What do you got there?" Pointing at Colson's journal, I lower my eyes to the small book and then back to Arno before I ask him the question I've been dying to ask him for more than a year now.

"What were you doing at Stone Fortress that night?" The way Arno's body stiffens at my question shows me it's a touchy subject for him. He inhales a few long, deep breaths while closing his eyes and letting his head hang low. He takes a few more breaths, and I wait patiently. I wasn't expecting this reaction from Arno. I thought maybe he would laugh at the thought or try to say something clever to deflect from the fact that he was at an auction for sex trafficking. However, his body language is full of pain as he battles an internal conflict within himself before answering me. I'm about to tell him never mind because clearly there is something deeper going on with him, but then he answers.

"I've been looking for a very important person for quite some time now." Arno lowers his head, closing his eyes and pinching the bridge of his nose as if it pains him to speak of whatever he's holding in. "A young woman, in fact." He lets out a small laugh before continuing. "It's funny, really. You remind me of her in some ways. Fearless, stubborn, always caring for others before herself, and clever. Fuck, she's clever." Arno pauses a moment, turning his head to look at me, his eyes showing just how much this woman means to him. "When I look at you, I see her, just like the first night I saw you. I actually thought you were her for a moment, the way you held your-self with such strength and certainty. I thought I'd found her." His voice lowers at his last comment, sadness permeating off his large frame, and my heart starts to ache for him.

"Well, that's why I was there. I was looking for someone very important to me. I've been going to Osiris's auctions ever since she was taken, in hopes I'd find her. As you can see, little one, I've had no such luck." Arno smiles at me, a smile that doesn't reach his eyes, and I'm lost at what to do to comfort him. Standing from where I'm sitting, I make my way over to him with outstretched arms. I grab hold of him, squeezing him tight hoping to comfort him with this simple gesture. Arno's massive stature pulls me in harder, cocooning me in his arms with a hug that speaks volumes. He's hurting, he's suffering, and I can't help but think I'm wasting his time here with me when he could be out there looking for whomever he's been searching for.

I stay locked in tight to his chest, both of us needing this embrace more than we even realized. After a long moment, we separate, and I step back, looking up at a man I thought I knew. From a monstrous, despicable, and vile human being to pulling back the veil of his true identity. Arno hides himself from everyone around him, protecting his heart and soul from destruction and pain that will eventually find us all. Arno's dark eyes are glossed over, holding back the tears he refuses to let go. Maybe this is the Shadow in him, never showing weakness and never admitting to pain, even when that pain is heartache.

"I don't need pity, Sloan. I understand the process of sex trafficking and I've come to terms with the inevitable. That won't stop me, however. I will continue my search, my hunt, and I will find her one way or another. And for those who took her...let's say the devil has a special place for them when I get through with them." The side of my lip curls up into a smile. If there's one thing I've learned from Arno, it's that he is a man of his word. Like the brotherly figure he is, Arno rubs the top of my head, disheveling my hair into a crazy mess.

"Come, let's get in a workout. I have some steam I need to blow off." I nod my head once and turn to grab Colson's journal before following after him. We reach the long hallway, and my curiosity takes hold of me.

"Arno, what's her name? The woman you're looking for?" His footsteps stop abruptly. The long hallway in front of us grows quiet with the absence of our footsteps. Arno tilts his head to the ceiling, letting out a long breath.

"You want to know her name, little one?" he asks me without turning around. "Only if you want to share with me," I whisper to him. "Her name—her name is Willow." With that, he continues down the hallway until he pushes through the gym doors, disappearing from my view.

Willow.

Her name is Willow.

Looking down at the journal, I squeeze it tightly between my fingers, having read that exact name from a previous entry Colson had written. She's alive, she's safe, and Colson saved her. I sprint down the hallway, placing my hand on the door, but freeze. What if this is not the right Willow? What if I get Arno's hopes up for nothing? I can't cause any more heartache for this man—my friend, my brother.

I will find this Willow for Arno and make sure this is who he's hunting for before I tell him. I can't hurt him, not anymore. I hope and pray to whoever's listening that this is his Willow.

CHAPTER 23

SLOAN

After putting Colson's journal back in Everett's office, I made my way back to the gym where Arno and I have been working out for the past hour. We've been working on more fighting techniques on the mat with the music blaring at max volume. "Limits" by Bad Omens rings in my ears as Arno lunges at me again. I dodge his hold, spinning away from his arms and positioning myself behind him once again. With his back to me, I see the rise of his shoulders as if he's chuckling to himself.

"You're getting pretty good at dodging me, little one. I'll give ya that." I smile to myself, pride filling my chest, when suddenly the gym doors burst open. Arno and I stand straight up, staring at Everett and Dean, who look like they've just seen a ghost. We all stand utterly still, Arno and I breathing heavily from training. Everett and Dean are breathing heavily from whatever news they just found.

"He's alive," Everett all but whispers to the room. The only reason we're able to hear him is because the music has ended and it's in between tracks. My eyes bounce back from Everett's to Dean's. The look in their eyes is one of pure relief. Out of the corner of my eye, I see Arno turn around to look at me. "Savior" by Rise Against blares through the speakers and I fall to my knees.

He's alive.

Colson is alive.

My head falls into my hands, and the floodgates completely open at the news. Sob after sob heaves from my chest, and I don't even realize when Dean wraps me in his arms.

"He's alive, baby girl, he's alive. We wouldn't have known if it weren't for you," Dean's voice whispers in my ear, his warm breath sending chills down my spine. They let me cry, all three of them as we're all kneeling on the wrestling mat. A hand rubs my back as I continue to heave my cries into Dean's chest. After far too long of me crying hysterically, I begin to collect myself, calming my breathing and wiping my tear-covered face with a gym towel. Everett hands me a water bottle and I twist the cap, chugging half the bottle.

"How do you know?" I ask the guys, my voice raspy from crying so hard. Dean looks to Everett, and I follow his gaze, awaiting his response.

"We were able to infiltrate their security cameras on the compound. Once we were in, we scanned every available live feed we could, until we found this." Everett raises his phone, the screen displaying what looks to be a live feed. I step closer to the phone, squinting to try to make out what exactly I'm looking at.

I'm looking at a dark, empty room—no windows, no furniture, nothing at all. Except for a single person, a man, kneeling on the floor shirtless, his arms extended above his head and to the sides. Long blond hair covers most of his back, but when the man turns his head sideways, a gasp slips from my lips.

"Colson," I whisper. Colson's arms are being held up by ropes tied to circular bars hanging from the far end of the room. My hand covers my mouth at the state of Colson. His once toned and muscular physique is now emaciated, every rib in his back noticeable with every breath he takes. His beautiful golden skin is now an ashen white, as if he hasn't stepped foot outside in six months. There's dried blood caked on the side of his neck that trails down his left side. His wrists being held by the ropes are bleeding, the rope tearing into his skin from being suspended for God knows how long.

Tears fall from my eyes as I examine the state of my once-full-of-life Colson. His frame is almost unrecognizable from the abuse, torture, and starvation he's been enduring for the past six months. My heart is breaking into a million pieces as the thought of me causing his pain flood my head. I let my emotions take hold of me, not allowing myself to see the decoy who was clearly not my Colson. If I'd kept a level head, I could've seen the signs. They were plain as day. How could I have been so stupid?

Clutching the phone in my hand, I start to tremble, anger coursing through my veins. The desire to destroy those who've done this to him clouding my vision. The once clear image of Colson in front of my eyes is now fading and the sharp edges of his outline blur until all I see is a distorted image I can no longer make out.

I hand the phone back to Everett, lifting my head to peer into his green eyes.

"What do we need to do to get him back?" My voice no longer sounds like my own. A wave of pure determination washes over my body, stiffening my muscles and gripping my chest in an uncomfortable, almost painful, hold. I watch as Everett and Dean exchange a hard look, silent communication flowing between them. I feel Arno step up beside me as I impatiently wait for their response.

I want to scream; I want to rip apart their organization from the inside out. I want them to beg for death after what I plan to do to each and every one of those who touched Colson. No one is getting out of this alive.

"Come with us. We've got an idea. But we need to move fast," Dean says to Arno and me before turning and exiting the gym. The rest of us follow close behind.

The four of us enter the office, Everett taking his seat behind his desk, where Dean and I sit on the leather sofa against the wall. Arno takes up the seat in front of Everett's desk, stretching out his long legs in front of him.

"Alright, mate, what do we need to do?" Arno speaks first, eager to hear what plan my guys have devised to rescue Colson. Everett turns his monitor towards us before enhancing what looks to be a blueprint of the compound where Colson is being held. I squint to get a better look at the map. Six red dots are actively moving around the outskirts of the compound.

"What are those dots indicating?" I ask, pointing at the screen. Dean answers me by adjusting his position on the couch, so he's turned towards me.

"We've already got Shadows on the ground. The moment we discovered Colson was alive, we sent them over. They're to remain on the border of the compound. Their main mission is to observe and report back to us if Colson is moved for any reason. They arrived on the ground roughly five hours ago."

"Smart. So, what's the plan for the extraction?" Arno asks, rubbing his hand through his hair. There is a long pause in the room, Dean and Everett not making eye contact with me. My blood starts to boil with the silence and the lack of communication they're giving me.

"What is it?" I say louder than I meant to. Time is ticking and we have no more extra time at this point. Colson has been suffering for far too long and without us, he's as good as dead. Everett lets out a long breath, closing his eyes and rubbing his hand down his face.

"We've been discussing possible options, however..." he stops, rolling his head to the side and cracking his neck.

"Out with it, mate," Arno says, waving his hand at Everett in a rushing motion. The expression Everett gives Arno could quite possibly kill if he stares at him long enough.

"What he's trying to say is, we've got a plan, but it's far too risky," Dean speaks up from beside me. I turn to face him, raising my eyebrows and waiting to hear this "far too risky" plan of theirs.

"For fuck's sake, spit it out, mate," Arno stands from his chair, frustration etched across his face.

"We send in a decoy of our own, play them at their own game," Everett finally says. Glancing down at the floor, I ponder what he means. Sending in a decoy, meaning sending in Everett who will pretend to be his twin brother Callum. It's smart, yes, they would never see it coming. To play one in their own game, switching the chess pieces and scrambling their playing board. I can't say I hate the idea, but yes, it is very risky. Sending anyone into that compound alone once again, let alone Everett for the second time, is not something I feel comfortable with. I can't see my guys being hurt any more than they already have. This is my family, my dream of having blood relatives and my own selfish desires landed all three of them in their own personal hell. No, I won't let that happen anymore.

Leaning back on the sofa, I close my eyes tight and try to think of a plan that eliminates the possibility of anyone else getting hurt, captured, tortured, or possibly killed. No one dies because of me. This is my fight, my war, my revenge. I sit up abruptly, an idea flooding my system.

"I've got an idea," I say to the room. All eyes are on me as my breathing picks up in nervous excitement at what I'm about to say. No one is going to like this, and if I'm able to convince them to go along with this plan, it will be a fucking miracle. I take in a deep breath before looking at each of them one more time before speaking again.

"How about we send me in, give them what they want most? Blind them with the prize, giving you enough time to get Colson out."

"Absolutely fucking not!" Dean yells from beside me, standing up and balling his fists by his side.

I expected that reaction.

CHAPTER 24

DEAN

Has she lost her ever-loving mind? For her to even think we would let her just walk into the largest organized crime family and offer herself up for slaughter, is the most idiotic thing I've ever heard. I'm fuming, my skin feels like it's on fire, and my palms are starting to hurt by how hard I'm squeezing my fists. No, I already lost my brother for the past six months because of this psychotic family. I'm not losing the only woman I've ever loved to these monsters.

Sloan has come a long way. She's strong, cunning, and so fucking smart, but with someone like Cara, I can't ensure her safety within the confines of the compound. I won't allow this; I can't lose her. Not now, not ever.

Looking at Everett, I notice he has yet to say a word. His cool demeanor not giving anything away.

He narrows his eyes at me, his eyebrows pinched ever so slightly together as if he is actually entertaining this idea.

"Well, mate, speak up. Tell her this idea is nothing more than an idea. We'll not allow this." His eyes shift to Sloan, his lip curling up as if he wants to hate the idea, but something is brewing in his own mind. "Everett, don't you fucking dare think about it!" I bark at him, stretching my arms to the side in disbelief.

"Dean, I agree with you. I don't like it either. But —" I point a finger at him, cutting him off.

"No, no buts, Everett, this is insane, and you know it. How can you sit there and even for one second think that sending our girl into hell would be a good idea? You were there, my friend. You saw and felt what they are capable of, and don't think just because she's a woman they would take it easy on her. If you're really thinking this is a good idea, why don't you take a look at this." Pulling my shirt over my head, I turn my back to him, showing him the evidence of the destruction they are capable of. My back is riddled with scars; some are still bright red with freshly regenerated skin. That was my punishment most of the time while we were imprisoned there. I was whipped over and over again until the pain became too much for my brain and body to process. I would soon slip away into the peace of being absent from my own body and fall unconscious.

I drop my shirt to the floor and glare at my girl. She, however, is not looking up at me. She is still seated on the sofa, her head lowered to the floor, hiding her face from the darkness that is me. I stomp out of the room, not wanting to say something I would surely regret. Heading towards the staircase, I take two at a time until I'm standing in front of Colson's room. His door is open, everything still where it was before we were captured. We've not changed a thing. His bed, dresser, lounge chair, everything sits where it sat the last time he was here.

My chest becomes so tight I feel as though I can't breathe. I finally unclench my fists, blood rushing back to each one of my fingers. I lift them to my face, rubbing my shaved head with both hands. They're shaking, as is the rest of my body. Anger, fear, heartache, my emotions are so jumbled up, it's as though I'm looking through a kaleidoscope.

I always knew this life we've been tossed into would be our undoing. I knew we would never live forever; something would inevitably go wrong, leaving one of us trapped or dead. I just always hoped it would be me instead of either of my brothers. The thought of living a life without one of them is too hard for me to process. A life without my brothers is a life not worth living in my mind. But then there is Sloan. A literal angel sent from the heavens to show me life is more than just bloodshed. She's the light.

No, she will not be thrown to the wolves as a

distraction for us to get Colson out. There are too many uncertainties and room for errors. I'm absolutely sure I would not be able to live a single moment without her. I won't risk it. Call me selfish, but when you're given a savior from above, you protect her at all costs, and I know Colson would say the same.

I don't hear her footsteps; I don't even hear her approach me, so when she wraps her arms around my back, resting her hands on my chest, I flinch at the sudden contact. Her delicate hands are so small they barely cover my pecs. Her soft touch is warm against my skin, and I close my eyes. Sloan has this power of calming me down without having to say or actually do anything. Her touch alone brings me tranquility, and whatever darkness that was swirling around my head suddenly vanishes.

"I can do this, Dean. I'm not the same girl you rescued that day. Let me help, let me bring him home to us. You've taught me so much. Let me prove it to you." Her words are a dagger to my heart. I know she can do this; I know how hard she's been training, and I have no doubt she can accomplish anything that's placed before her. But I can't lose her.

"Baby girl, I can't—" My voice shakes, and I suck in a deep breath, calming the war that's starting to brew inside once again. "If anything were to happen to you, I wouldn't be able to walk this earth knowing you're no longer here with me. You're not just my girl, Sloan. You're the air inside my lungs, the blood pumping in my heart, you're my whole existence." I turn to face her, her hands falling from my chest as I turn to see tears forming in her eyes. Cupping her face, I rest my forehead on hers.

"A life without you is a life I don't want to live."

CHAPTER 25

SLOAN

I close my eyes as Dean pulls me to his lips, kissing me with so many unspoken words. He's scared, I can feel it. The thought of losing me to the monsters that tortured him is more than he can bear. Dean's love is palpable, his touch giving away just how much I mean to him. Love is just a word; I've always found it silly to say a four-letter word to someone to describe the intense emotion I'm feeling from within. Rather than say such a small, simple word, I would rather have someone show me their love, and vice versa.

That's how Dean shows me his feelings for me. Dean's slowly pulling our bodies into Colson's room, our lips never leaving one another's. Standing at the end of the bed, I'm suddenly spun around until the backs of my legs are up against the mattress. He continues to devour me, his hands roaming every inch of my body. As I go to wrap my arms around his neck, he pulls away. The warmth of his lips leave mine, and the sudden absence of his body leaves me wobbling on my feet.

His hand wipes down his face, the internal conflict of our conversation downstairs raging war inside his mind.

"You're not going, Sloan. I won't let you throw yourself to the lions for Colson, for Everett, for me. I can't allow them to hurt you." Dean's voice is stern, his tone low and deep. As he speaks, he begins to pace the room in front of me.

"I will, Dean," I whisper back to him. My voice is shaky as I stand up to him. I've been told what to do my whole life. "This is the only way I see that we can get Colson back. If that means I have to put myself in danger, then I'll do it."

"No! I won't let you." Dean steps up to my face, looking down at me with ferocity in his eyes. Gone is the sweet Dean, and here stands the Dean with darkness oozing out from within.

Standing on my tiptoes, I gently place my hand over his collarbone and glide my hand up to the side of his neck. I stop at the side of his face and slowly rub my thumb along his jawline. His eyes close to my touch, his once heavy breathing finally coming to a regular rhythm.

"Why don't you show me your love for you?" My words come out in a whisper as he leans his head into my hand. Not opening his eyes, he responds to my question.

"I can't lose you too." My heart aches at this comment. Besides Everett and myself, Dean has lost everyone he has ever been able to call family. We are the only ones he has. Losing Colson was the hardest thing he and Everett ever had to endure. The thought of losing me is too painful. Not allowing me to go is his way of protecting me, showing me he loves me.

"You won't lose me; I've been trained by the best. You have to trust in your training skills that you've prepared me enough to handle myself. I trust you. Now you have to trust me." When his eyes open, sadness stares back at me. The pupils that swirled with shadows and fury are now hollow empty orbs, allowing me to see straight into his soul. I lean in and kiss his soft lips, holding my face to his for a long moment. As I release my lips from his, I pull his head to mine until our foreheads meet.

"If throwing myself to the lions ensures we get Colson back, I'm doing it. I'd do it for you, I'd do it for Everett. Why? Because I know without a shadow of a doubt the three of you would burn this world down to rescue me."

"You better fucking believe we would, baby girl." Grabbing my ass, he lifts me from the floor and throws me onto the bed. Before I can raise up on my elbows, his hard body is on top of mine. He spreads my legs with his knee, settling himself between my thighs. I groan as he grinds himself against my aching center, the bulge in his pants rubbing against my leggings. There is suddenly far too much clothing between the both of us. I want nothing more than to be stripped away from the confines of these fabrics. I reach for Dean's jeans button, but he pulls away from me again.

"You have to promise me something first," he says, giving me a devilish glare. I raise an eyebrow at him, wondering what he has planned, when all I want him to do right now is help satisfy the throbbing between my legs.

"What's that?"

"If I allow you to go in as a decoy, we do it my way. No exceptions." I can see there's no other way around this. Dean won't let me do this alone. I never thought he would. Instead of saying anything, I give him a single nod of my head.

"That's not good enough, baby. I need to hear you say it. Say 'I promise'." This man is insufferable. I get where he's coming from, I really do. I hated watching my men leave me at the castle, not knowing if things would go south. Spoiler alert—things did. But if he'll let me do this with a few stipulations, so be it.

"I promise, Dean." With that, Dean's hands slide up my shirt, pulling the fabric up and over my head. His lips trail down my front, kissing his way between my breasts and down my abdomen. When he reaches the top of my leggings, he stops, grabbing the sides and yanking them down my legs. He moves fast, like a feral animal pouncing on his prey. As I pull my legs out of the prison of my leggings, Dean freezes, staring down at my body until his eyes reach mine.

"If heaven is a person, it'd most certainly be you, baby girl." Crashing his body against mine, he kisses me again, inhaling me with every swipe of his tongue. The bed dips beneath me, and the warmth of Dean's body against mine is suddenly gone. He stands, quickly making work of his pants, freeing himself from the confines of his jeans. As he stands beside the bed, I stare at the man before me. Dean has never missed a day in the gym. It's evident with every move he makes, his muscles flexing beneath his tight skin. He's beautiful. He takes pride in his health, his work, and being ready at a moment's notice to carry out whatever mission the corporation assigns him. He went from being a broken kid on the streets to throwing himself in this world in hopes of being a part of something, being a part of a family, a family he never had.

I admire this man. Standing in the dark of the room, his silhouette stalks beside the bed, looking down at my body, at his own personal buffet.

"I can't and will never lose you, Sloan. You're mine and I'm yours. In this life and the next. No one is going to take you from me, you understand?" Shaking my head at him, he crawls back onto the bed, straddling my hips once more. Pinning my hands above my head, he awaits my response, his dark eyes burning straight through my chest, making my heart beat faster.

"I'm yours. Now and forever."

DEAN

This woman—this insufferably beautiful, stubborn woman—will be the death of me. This, I'm sure of. Besides my brothers, I have never felt this strong of a desire to protect another human being as I do with her. She is my main and only focus. I want to put her in a cage, lock her in my room and never let her go. I can't bear the thought of her being hurt, being tortured, or, dare I say, killed. I won't let that happen. Looking down at her now, I want to strangle her for even suggesting she would be a decoy. Leaning down so my mouth brushes against her ear, I whisper, "Don't think for one second you won't be punished for this little hero stunt of yours. Everyone else may be okay with allowing you to walk into the darkness, but you forget who already resides in the shadows." Her breath hitches as she takes in my words. I promise she will regret making that suggestion before the night is over. Darting my tongue out, I lick up the side of her face, the taste of her sweet skin sending my senses into a frenzy.

Holding her immobile, I reach beneath the bed and pull out my rope I've placed under Colson's bed. Something I've done strategically for moments like these. Her eyes grow wide when she sees what I've retrieved. I don't miss the slight twitch of her lip showing me just how much she likes being tied down. Wrapping the rope around her wrists, I make sure they're extra tight, pinching her skin just a little tighter than necessary.

When I finish with her wrist, I latch back onto her neck with my lips, kissing and licking my way down her chest and spending extra time at her breasts. Taking her nipple in my mouth, I bite down just enough to make her back bow. She hisses through her teeth, and just when I think she may cry out, I kiss away the pain, her body melting back into the mattress.

"My girl likes the pain, don't you?" I muse, already knowing the answer. A soft moan bubbles up from her chest, her head giving me a slight nod.

"That's my good girl." Kissing my way down her toned abdomen, I can feel her tensing muscles as I slowly reach the spot she's dying for me to touch. Pulling away from her stomach, I hover my lips over her eager pussy, looking up at her face. I can see the neediness in her eyes as she peers down at me.

"You want me to relieve that ache for you, baby girl?" I taunt her, the look in her eyes pleading with me. I open my mouth, keeping my eyes locked on hers as I lower my face towards her core. Just when I'm about to lick the spot she wants me to most, I close my lips and blow warm air over her sensitive spot. Her thighs twitch, and she moans as the sensation sends shivers throughout her body.

"Ugh, please, Dean, please," she begs me. I smile

to myself, knowing how much she aches to be touched.

"You thought I'd make this easy for you? I told you; your little stunt will not go unpunished. I'm in control right now, and I say when you cum." Just when she starts lifting her head off the bed to give me a death glare, I rise from the bed, grab another one of my stashed ropes, and begin securing her legs together. When I've successfully tied up my clever girl. I lean down to her ear once more and whisper, "Now, you'll sit here until you've learned just how much you drive me crazy." I kiss the side of her face and leave her tied up on the bed, locking Colson's room behind me. As I'm walk down the hall I hear her scream, "Dean, don't you fucking leave me here! Dean!" I chuckle to myself continuing down the stairs, her screams fading away behind me.

That'll teach her.

CHAPTER 26

DEAN

Making my way to the guys downstairs, I hear their faint chatter in the kitchen as I enter the room. Both Everett and Arno turn to face me, their eyes darkening when they hear a faint scream coming from upstairs.

"Why the fuck is she screaming, Dean?" Everett asks me, his eyes fixed over my head in the direction of her pleads. My lips pull in a side smile as I make my way to the fridge, pulling it open and grabbing a beer. Popping the top, I turn to face them again, noticing the small smile Arno is trying to conceal but not doing a good job.

"Dean?" Everett asks again. I ignore his question, rounding the island and pulling out a bar stool, sitting down and taking a large swig of my beer. Setting it on the island, I clear my throat.

"Never mind her—she's learning a quick lesson.

Now, we have to discuss what this whole decoy plan is about and how we are going to ensure she is safe at all times." Arno lets out a laugh, shaking his head in disbelief, as Everett gives me a glare of disapproval. Everett also shakes his head and closes his eyes as he brushes his hair back with both hands.

"She's going to be so pissed at you, mate," Arno says through his deep chuckles. I don't give a fuck how pissed she is with me; like I promised her, she wasn't getting off easy.

"Nothing new, mate. Now, back to the question at hand. How is she going to be a decoy, walk into the Irish mob, not be captured and tortured, or even killed? Tell me how you thought that was a good idea, brother?" I'm glaring right at Everett as I ask this question. My heart starting to race at the idea of her being captured by Cara.

However, it's not Everett who answers me, it's Arno.

"Because I'll be there with her the whole time." My eyes dart to the big man, not seeing how that was going to ensure her safety, but okay. I wait for him to continue, the confusion evident on my face.

"While you were playing your fuck-fuck games upstairs, Everett and I were talking. Cara doesn't know me; she doesn't know my connection with her or with you two. The only other person who knows me within their organization is Cal. The one thing Cal does know is my hatred for the three of you. The last he saw of me was in training and at that time we were all mortal enemies, in case you forgot." I take another swig of my beer, wondering where his thought process is going. My eyes shift from Arno to Everett, he raises an eyebrow at me, his silent way of telling me to just fucking listen to the plan.

"I take Sloan as my prisoner, giving Cara what she wants most, the last known heir to the Wallace family. While she is distracted with us, the two of you get Colson to safety, all while the perimeter is being secured until we are able to launch our attack on Cara, Cormick, and Cal."

I take another swig of my beer, enjoying the ice-cold liquid as I take in this new plan. It's a good plan. Yes. I don't, however, want to admit that this plan could possibly work. I don't want to agree to this, because that means Sloan goes into the viper's nest and that's the last thing I want her to do.

"Stop acting like you're going to think of a better plan, mate, and just fucking say yes already. Time is ticking." The glare I give Arno could melt the flesh right off his bones. The arrogant son of a bitch telling me we have no more time, when it's my brother that needs rescuing.

"Don't act like you care for Colson more than I do, mate." I emphasize the last word, letting him know how much his comment just pissed me off.

"Listen, you two. Don't start with your bullshit. This is the plan; I've already let the other Shadows know and have already started packing up and getting into position." I look at Everett, rage settling under my skin, knowing he's already agreed to a plan I haven't had a fucking say in. This is our girl we're talking about!

"You think Sloan is going to agree without hearing the plan first?"

"Yes, I'm in."

As if I couldn't be backed into a tighter corner, my skin tightens over my flexed muscles as I look over my shoulder and see her. She's standing in the doorway, one hand clenching the ropes that were just tightly secured around her arms and legs, the other hand pointed right at me.

She looks stunning even when she's heaving with anger. Her long blond hair is disheveled, her chest rapidly rising and falling through each angry breath. However, her anger is not what has me speechless at the moment. It's the fact that she's standing there, clenching the ropes and very much naked.

Fuck, she's perfect.

CHAPTER 27

SLOAN

If this fucking caveman thinks for one second, tying me up and leaving me in Colson's room will stop me from helping, he's got another thing coming. The moment I was able to slip one of my hands out from Dean's poor excuse of a knot, I was able to free myself completely. Has he forgotten who's been training me for the last six months? Plot twist, it's been him!

I was going to get dressed before heading downstairs to strangle Dean, but my rage has taken over. I am so infuriated I kick open the bedroom door and practically run down the hallway, stark naked. Fuck it. Clothes can wait. Plus, I want to see the look on Dean's face when he sees I was able to escape his piss-poor knots. Frankly, it's laughable. As I make my way down the stairs, I round the banister and head straight for the kitchen. Before I make my presence known, I hear Arno talking about some plan. A plan that involves me being a decoy—exactly what I suggested before. Do these men ever listen? The moment I hear Dean ask if I would agree to this plan, I step through the doorway and agree. Butt ass naked.

"The fuck, little one? You trying to burn my eyes out of their sockets?" Arno barks before turning around to shield his eyes from me. I toss the ropes on the floor in front of Dean with a heavy thud.

"Do you really think I wouldn't be able to get out of those?" I point to the ropes, expecting Dean to look furious, but the heat in his eyes tells me something different.

"I hoped you'd escape, because if you didn't, you could've kissed your decoy plan goodbye." Dean's voice is all sexy as his eyes look at my legs and slowly roam up my body. I clench my legs together, seriously regretting my decision to be naked. The throbbing between my legs is harder to hide when I can't hide behind clothes. Fuck. As if he can sense my regret, the corner of Dean's mouth tilts up in a devilish smirk. With two long strides, Dean is suddenly standing right in front of me, his gray eyes staring down at me with nothing but lust heat my core.

"I've underestimated your abilities, baby girl." Brushing a strand of hair behind my ear, his fingers graze my neck, sending shivers throughout my body. "Now you understand the risk you'll be taking with this plan?" His voice is low, and I can tell he's worried. I nod my head as I rest my cheek in his large palm.

"I can do this, Dean. You have to trust that you've taught me well." He releases a deep sigh, accepting the fact that he won't win this battle.

"Fine, we leave in the morning, but first I have to finish what I started." Grabbing me by the waist, Dean hoists me over his shoulder causing me to let out a small squeak of surprise. Carrying me towards the stairs, I look up at Everett, his handsome lips pulling to one side before he mouths, "You're mine next." I shoot him a wink and blow him a kiss, excited about what my guys have in store for me. Before we round the corner, I catch a glimpse of Arno. He's turned back around, but his hands are still firmly covering his eyes. I chuckle to myself, realization dawning that I probably traumatized him. Like he's never seen a naked woman before.

Dean takes the stairs two at a time, mumbling how he's going to punish me for Arno seeing me naked or something along those lines. As he kicks open Colson's door, he tosses me on the bed flat on my back. With his heavy boot, Dean kicks the door closed behind him, staring down at me with murderous intent. I give him a smirk, wanting him to do his worst. I've been wound up since he first tied me up. I'm aching for a release.

Dean undoes his belt, pulling the leather out of the loops and snapping the belt off his hand, making my pussy throb even more. Stalking towards the bed, he pulls his shirt over his head with one hand, making my pulse rise.

"You think that was funny, do you, giving Arno a free show of what's mine?" I don't answer him. I simply shrug my shoulders as I prop myself on my elbows. "I see, you want to play that game?" Biting my lower lip, I watch as he unbuttons his pants, the sound of the zipper echoing through the room. "I'll show you what'll happen if you do that again."

Before he can make another move, I lift myself up so I'm sitting off the edge of the bed directly in front of him. I grab his jeans before he can pull them down and pull his large frame even closer to me.

"Here, let me apologize." Grabbing the hem of his briefs, I free his already erect cock, and it springs free in front of me. My eager hands waste no time. I grab him at the base, spit on his shaft, and start pumping ever so slowly.

"Fuckkkk," Dean growls, letting his head fall back as I continue to pump. Watching as he comes undone in front of me, I want to see more. Licking my lips, I open my mouth to him, taking in his soft head and wrapping my lips around his hard length. Looking up at him as I continue to take him deeper down my throat, his abdomen flexes, making me smile internally.

"Thatta girl, take all of me," he groans, his fingers threading through my hair and pushing me deeper until I can feel him pushing against the back of my throat. My eyes start to water at his enormous length, but I keep him there, swallowing him down to keep me from gagging.

"You take me so well." His hand starts to pull my hair back, my lips sliding against his velvety smooth length until he's completely free, my lips making a popping sound as he pulls out of me. Dean tilts my chin up so he can see my whole face, saliva dripping down my chin. With his thumb, he cleans away the drool from my chin.

"So, fucking beautiful when you're choking on my cock." I let out a moan of satisfaction with his praise. I open my mouth once again, sticking my tongue out in an invitation to choke me some more. Just as the tip touches my tongue, the bedroom door flies open, startling me. Sitting back on the bed, I see the silhouette of a man, breathing heavily as he reaches for the door, closing it with a loud slam.

"Did you think you'd be the only one punishing her for that little show, mate?" The smooth yet dangerous tone of Everett's voice has me clenching my thighs together. My pussy throbs, the need and desire for more friction between my legs causing me to burn up.

"She was just showing me how sorry she is," Dean says to Everett, his hand threading back through my hair and lining my lips up with his cock once more.

"Perfect. I need an apology as well. No one sees our girl naked but us." Stepping into the room further, Everett stands beside Dean, unbuttoning his trousers. Once finished, he rips open the front of his button-up shirt, causing buttons to fly and exposing his flexed abs. Fuck, these men are giving me exactly what I want.

As I stare at Everett's chest, Dean, without warning, pushes his cock down my throat in a harsh thrust, making my eyes water. Dean is moaning with his satisfaction as he sets a rhythm, pushing my head up and down his cock, my lips greedily sucking as he goes.

"Look how sorry she is, mate," Dean groans to Everett. I grab onto Dean's thigh to steady myself, but it's not long before I find my knees on the floor, peering up at him as I swallow his cock.

"I'm still waiting for my apology, love." My eyes look up to see Everett. His cock is already out while his hand is pumping long, lazy strokes down his length. The tension Dean has on my hair eases up and I'm able to pop my lips off the end of his cock. Licking the mess off my lips, I let go of Dean's thighs. I grab onto Everett's, pulling him closer to me so I can take him into my mouth. Grabbing the base of his cock in my hand, I spit on the tip before wrapping my lips around him and taking him to the back of my throat.

"Baby girl," Everett drawls, his deep voice giving me all the praise I need. I continue my way up and down his length, his cock twitching between my lips as my speed picks up. "Yes, love, take it all. Be a good girl for me." Saliva drips down my chin, my lips sucking and popping off his tip every time I pull out.

"Keep going, beautiful, don't move," I hear Dean say from behind me. I didn't even notice when he moved from Everett's side. Dean's large hands grab my waist, lifting my ass up so high I have to place both my hands on Everett's thighs to steady myself. Everett grabs my hair in a tight fist, pulling me all the way into him, his cock pushing on the back of my throat, my face buried against his lower stomach. Just when I feel like I can't hold my breath anymore, he pulls me away from him. I gasp for air, but I only get a couple of deep breaths before he pulls me forward once again, his cock pushing past my lips.

Dean still has a hand on my waist, as he rubs my ass with the other. His fingers coming so close to the spot I'm dying for him to touch. Pushing back towards him, he lets out a low groan.

"Is this what you want, baby girl, for me to touch you here?" Dean's fingers brush over my most sensitive spot, his fingers barely brushing the ache between my legs. I moan, continuing to push back, needing him to give me some relief. "Then you better promise us you won't pull that shit again. Like Everett said, no one sees our girl naked but us. You belong to us." I moan again, my mouth too full of Everett's cock to answer him, so hopefully my moans will tell him just how much I promise. "Thatta girl," he coos from behind me, two fingers slowly pushing past my lips and into my eager pussy. I moan around Everett's cock, his abdomen flexing with the vibration of my moans.

"Fuckkk, mate, she's very, very sorry," Everett says to Dean. "Should we give her what she wants?"

he asks, my eyes widening at the need for Dean, for Everett—fuck—for both of them. "Right, then, fill her up, mate." With that, Dean thrusts his cock fully inside me, the pain of his cock stretching my walls morphing into a delicious pleasure. Everett pulls my hair, his cock popping off my lips again. He pats the side of my cheek a couple times, my breathing trying to catch up from switching from one cock to the other.

"Good girl," he coos down at me, but I'm lost in the friction of Dean's cock inside me I can't focus on anything else. Everett kneels down in front of me so his face is level with mine, his lips capturing mine in a brutal kiss. Our tongues entangle as Dean continues thrusting from behind me. I moan into Everett's mouth. When Dean hits the spot inside me, my core buzzes with a building orgasm.

"She's close, mate," Everett calls to Dean over my head. "That makes two of us." Dean's pace picks up, his thrusts hard and fast as Everett stands to his feet once again. Stepping closer to me, Everett grabs his cock and rubs the tip over my lips.

"Open wide, love." I do as I'm told, my tongue darting out as he pushes the head past my lips until I'm gagging on his length once again. Everett places both his hands on my head, his fingers gripping my hair as he finds his rhythm.

I'm so close, my thighs and abs are flexed so tight as I chase my orgasm. When Dean presses his thumb against my clenched hole, I detonate. The floor is wobbling beneath me as black spots cloud my vision.

The heat between my legs sends shock waves throughout my body as my walls clamp around Dean's cock.

"Fuck yes, just like that," Dean says, his hands grabbing my waist and squeezing tight. A few thrusts later, Dean finds his release, filling me up as he groans with his pleasure.

"My fucking turn." Is all the warning I get. Everett pushes his cock so far down my throat, holding me there until warm jets of cum slide down the back of my throat. When he finishes, he pulls my hair back, his already softening cock sliding from my throat. I greedily gasp for air as drool and remnants of Everett slide down my chin. Dean then pulls out of my pussy, his warm seed sliding down my thighs. I'm a mess, an utter mess of drool, cum, and the most delicious post-orgasmic bliss I could ever ask for.

I almost fall to the floor as soon as Dean is fully out of me, but his large arms wrap around my waist, holding me to his hard front as I continue to find my breath. Leaning back on Dean, I hear the sound of running water. Opening my eyes, I see Everett exiting the bathroom, billows of steam following after him. Standing in front of me, he grabs my chin with his thumb.

"You, my dear, look like you could use a shower." I don't respond. I don't even move my legs towards the shower. Dean laughs from over my shoulder as he scoops me up in his arms and carries me to the bathroom. Placing me down softly, Everett enters the shower first, helping me step beneath the overhead facet as Dean makes his way in behind me. The three of us shower, both my guys cleaning me softly as I lean into them. I let my head wander, thoughts of Colson being here soon making me smile.

The four of us. Soon we'll be complete.

CHAPTER 28

SLOAN

After my so-called punishments, we all fell asleep naked in Colson's bed. However, I couldn't fall asleep right away. The thoughts of Colson being back in this room—his room—in his bed with me, had my mind racing with excitement. The next morning, we met up with Arno, Stefan, and Jei to go over the plan in more elaborate detail. Looking through our entrance points on the map of the compound and where Arno and I would be offering myself up as the decoy. I'd be lying if I said I wasn't scared. I mean, damn, I was about to offer myself up to Cara. The bitch, who not only stole my men from me, but has also been torturing Colson for the past six fucking months. As scared as I am about this plan, my desire for revenge surpasses all fears that lurk beneath my surface.

Everett and Dean have a very small window where they will be able to sneak into the compound where Colson is being held, retrieve him, and retreat back to the "safe zone" before Arno's and my cover is discovered. My goal is to keep Cara talking for as long as possible. You know those movies where the villain has a long monologue they spew right before they are taken out? Well, that's my goal. Keep her talking so my guys can get the third piece of my heart to safety. Sounds easy enough.

"Right, is everyone clear on what their objectives are? Anyone confused in any way? Speak up now. There is no room for fuck ups with this extraction." Everett slowly gazes around the room at the lot of us and watches each one of our heads nod in assurance.

"Right then, get your gear, and let's head out. Plane leaves in one hour." Arno claps my shoulder before exiting the room with Stefan, Jei, Stone, and Cane following behind him. I watch as their footsteps fade away and the front door closes loudly behind them. I inhale a deep breath, turning to look at Everett and Dean, who are both standing behind the office desk, watching me intently.

"What?" I ask, the heat of their gazes making my skin burn.

"You sure you want to do this, love?" Everett asks, his hands resting flat on the desk, all the while his eyes remain on mine. His brows are furrowed together, his emerald eyes darker than normal, as he waits for my response. My eyes fall on Dean, his huge arms are crossed over his chest, as he, too, stares at me with darkened eyes. I let out a short breath straightening my back as I say, "I've never been more sure about something in my life." I don't falter or give any indication that I'm even the slightest bit concerned. I'm ready to prove to myself that the once scared and frightened little girl who snuck up to the roof to escape those who once hurt me is gone. I've spent too much of my life cowering and running from the monsters that haunt me in the dark. The demons who slowly stripped me of my innocence, only to be tossed into the depths of misery. No. She's no longer with us. She's been altered, changed, reborn into what they will soon come to realize as their worst fucking nightmare.

"Let's stop wasting time. Let's go get him." I leave the room, heading upstairs to pack a small bag of essentials. I already know the guys have their arsenal of weapons packaged and ready for use. I, however, want to pack a few things for Colson, such as first aid supplies, some clean clothes, and his throw blanket he always had laid out on his bed. He'll want a sense of comfort and normalcy.

The hour flies by in a rush as the team and I grab what we need and make our way to the airstrip. Awaiting us is Arno and the rest of the team already loaded up and waiting for the three of us to arrive. Exiting the SUV, I take a moment and freeze as my gaze lands on the plane that I've seen so many times in my nightmares. The same small jet where I once saw Colson die, the same jet I relived that horrific day in the simulation. I close my eyes for a moment and say in my head, *This time will be different. We are all coming home. Alive.*

"Right, you all set, little one?" My eyes snap open to Arno, who's standing in front of me, a look of concern etched across his face. I nod once, straightening my back as I start towards the jet. He stops me, however, as his hand wraps around my bicep.

"You've got this. Get out of your head and harden the fuck up. Your man's waiting for you. Show them no mercy." With that, he lets my arm go, leaving me standing there as I absorb his words. I roll my shoulders as I make my way to the jet. Climbing the stairs and finding my seat, a seat far away from the place I remember holding Colson as he died in my arms.

Show them no mercy.

The plane is quiet; there's no chatter, no usual banter—nothing. Just a small space full of pissed off, revenge seeking Shadows who've been waiting to taste blood for quite some time now. If I were Cara, I'd be praying to whoever she prays to that death finds her quickly. I'm looking out the window when a strong hand rests on my thigh. Turning from the window, I see Everett sitting beside me as he studies my face. I sink further into my chair, allowing the plush leather to absorb my small frame.

"Here, this is for you." Everett extends his hand to me, slick metal filling his palm. It's a Glock 19—a 9mm semi-automatic pistol—the same pistol I've been training with for the past six months. This one's a little different. There's engraving on the side. Turning my head, I read it out loud.

"My Awakening." I look at Everett and see that Dean is now standing behind him, his towering frame filling the small space around us.

"They've awakened the lion in you, love. The caged animal they'll soon regret ever trying to silence. I saw the lion in your eyes the first night we brought you home. I told you then that you weren't meant to be caged, and seeing you grow the past few months signifies who you've become. The animal inside is coming to life and taking back what's yours." I give Everett a small smile, his words filling me with so much hope that this plan will succeed. This plan will bring my family together again. The four of us, well, five, including Arno, will soon be whole.

"As much as I don't want you in harm's way, you're ready for this. You've proven yourself over and over again," Dean says over Everett's head, his arms crossed over his chest. I finally take the pistol from Everett's hand, enjoying the cool metal between my fingers as I turn it over in my hands. It's smooth and slick. The feeling of power that engulfs my core is invigorating. I can do this. I've been training for this and right now I feel more dangerous than I've ever felt.

"Thank you," I say to both of them. My gaze is still on my new pistol as it fits perfectly in my hand.

"Just don't shoot me, little one, I mean it." I look up to see Arno leaning his head back towards me as he shoots me a wink before crossing his arms behind his head and eases back in the recliner. I smile to myself. The realization of what these men have done for me—trained me, prepared me for what's to come—makes the back of my eyes sting. Tucking the pistol behind me in my waist band I look up to my guys.

"Let's go get our boy, shall we?" The smiles Everett and Dean give me are pure admiration as they each take turns kissing my forehead before settling back into their chairs. Everett grabs my hand in his and intertwines our fingers together for the rest of the fight.

We're coming for you, Colson.

CHAPTER 29

SLOAN

We land roughly twenty-five minutes later, in a small field surrounded by trees. It's pitch-black outside, only the moon provides us with minimal light to help us see. Exiting the plane, I see that this is not the same field Arno and I landed in when we first came to get the guys. As if he could sense my realization, Arno comes up behind me, resting his hand on my shoulder.

"This isn't the same location as before; this is The Shadows' secured landing strip provided to us by one of the higher-ups. He bought this property about three years ago, allowing him to come and go to his private compound he's built upon his retirement. Once he heard about Colson, he gave us permission to use his land. Lucky for us, this air strip is only three hours from where the Wallace's compound is located." I nod once, as my eyes try to adjust to the darkness around us.

The guys begin unloading the plane, their large duffels piling on the damp grass in front of me.

"Right, everything's set," Everett says to me. Pulling out his cell, he clicks open his text messages. "Our ride will be here in two minutes."

"Good, it's fucking freezing out here," Arno says as he blows air into his hands, rubbing them together, trying to stay warm.

"Aww, you need a hug, mate?" Stefan jokes as he claps his hand on Arno's back.

"Yeah, I do actually. You gonna rub me down with your soft hands?" Arno fires back, their banter making me smile to myself.

"Alright, lovers, enough. Our ride's here," Dean chimes in, his tone serious as he tosses his duffle over his shoulder and makes his way over to a blacked-out suburban that's making its way from beneath the cover of the forest. I follow close behind him, my own bag slung over my shoulder as footsteps behind me tell me the rest are following.

As we pile into the suburban, I find myself squished in between Everett and Dean. Not complaining one bit because poor Jei is behind me squished in between Arno and Stefan. Chuckling to myself, I notice Stone is in the front passenger seat. I glance around for a moment, searching for where Cain is going to sit, and notice he's closing the back hatch door. Poor fella has to sit in the trunk, along with all the duffels.

"Thanks, mate, for allowing us to use your airstrip." Everett claps the shoulder of the driver.

"Not a problem, fellas, anything to still feel relevant in the organization. Don't know what to do with myself half the time, sitting at home twiddling my fucking fingers. I need a little action now and then," the driver laughs out. "I'm Stix, by the way, sweetheart. You must be Sloan." Our driver, Stix, turns to give me a head nod, and I return the gesture with a smile.

"Fuck, sorry, Stix. Yes, this is Sloan. Sloan, this is Stix," Everett says apologetically.

"It's a pleasure, and I can't thank you enough for helping us," I say quickly.

"Anytime, sweetheart. We never leave a man behind." I lower my head at that statement, because honestly? That's exactly what I did six months ago. I left Colson behind; he's been suffering the wrath of Cara because my stupidity and emotions blinded me from seeing the truth that was right in front of me. Simultaneously, Dean and Everett rest their hands on my thighs, each giving me a reassuring squeeze that Stix's comment was not a dig at my carelessness.

The drive is long, and my body soon betrays me as my eyelids become too heavy to keep open. I don't know how long I sleep for, but the sound of the guys bickering wakes me from my deep sleep. I keep my eyes shut, however, wanting to know what the guys are fussing about.

"I mean it, Arno, anything—and I mean anything—happens to her while she's with you and I promise to make your life a living fucking nightmare," Dean's familiar voice whispers beside me.

"Listen, mate, you know this job as well as I do. Nothing can ever be promised when it comes to someone's life. However, I assure you I will do everything in my power to keep her safe. You're not the only one who cares for her," Arno's voice whispers from behind me. He and I have become close since my guys were taken. He's been there for me, comforted me, and been that brother figure every little sister loves to hate. I trust him, and I wish Dean could trust him as I do. I know he wouldn't intentionally let anything happen to me. Arno's right, this world we live in is dangerous and nothing can be promised. The only thing we can do is our best.

"Dean, I have to intervene here and remind you how dangerous emotions can be in situations like these. You have to trust she knows what she's doing, because you've trained her, and remain focused on getting your brother out alive. Once that's accomplished, raise hell and get back to your girl. But remember, worrying about her the whole time will only get you killed, and she doesn't want your death on her hands." I don't entirely recognize who's talking, but the voice is coming from in front of me. That leaves Stone and Stix, and if I'd have to guess, it would be Stix. Stone is not the one to give heavy advice like this to Dean. This advice seems to come from someone with a lot more experience. My chest tightens for Dean and how concerned he is with my well-being.

He once told me, *"Love is cruel. The feeling itself makes me feel full, yet when distance becomes a factor for whatever reason, love hurts with the intensity of a volcano."*

At this very moment, I know all too well what he means. When they were taken, I couldn't breathe, I couldn't think straight. Rage was constantly boiling underneath my skin, and I couldn't fathom the idea of them being tortured the way they were. The way Colson has been this whole time. As hard as this will be for him, for both of them, I'm ready. I'm ready because I've been trained by the best.

"He's right, Dean," I interrupt, my head resting on his shoulder. "You have to trust in your own training. You've taught me how to kill someone in twelve different ways. Training I can't wait to unleash on my own fucked-up family." I lift my head and turn to face him. I rest my hand on his chest, feeling his heart pumping like a demon ready to be unleashed. "We all go home this time, alive." I lean forward and capture his lips with mine. His hand grabs hold of my face, holding me still to his. His lips are strong, forcing mine apart so he can taste my tongue with his.

"Alright, alright, let's not make my dick hard.

Lord knows I haven't used it in a long while," Stix interrupts us as Arno coughs behind me in disgust.

"Jesus, Stix, I didn't need that mental image, mate," Arno spits out between his gagging noises. The sound of Stix's laughter fills the car, while Dean continues to hold my face with his hand.

"Don't do anything stupid and reckless, baby girl. Get in, do the job, and get out. I'll be there as soon as I can."

"We will be there as soon as we can," Everett chimes in from beside me. My two men, my two possessive and protective knights in shining armor, always assuring me they'll be there for me. I believe them one hundred and ten percent.

"We all go home safe," I say to the pair of them, just as the suburban comes to a halt.

"Right, we've made it to phase one. Time to get your game faces on boys—and girl," Stix says.

Game on.

CHAPTER 30

SLOAN

"Arno and I drive the main road leading to the entrance to the compound. After checking in with security and making our presence known, we'll radio back to Stone and Cain so they can run the loop footage prior to us driving past the security camera located at the entrance," I address the group.

"Assuming the guards at the front alert Cara to our arrival, we predict she'll have all-hands-on-deck to ensure Sloan is in fact on the premises," Arno continues with the plan.

"While the two of them make their way to the front of the compound, Jei and I will take down the two security guards at the front. Then wait for Everett and Dean to arrive where we will all continue to phase two," Stefan says.

"Right, good. The moment Arno and Sloan pass the front guards, Dean and I will make our way to the building where we were held with Colson. We'll breach the building and make our way down the trapdoor and through the tunnel to the room where Colson is currently being held. We've seen there is always one guard posted at his door at all times. So, we eliminate him quietly and get Colson out. After following the tunnel back outside, Stone and Cain will be ready to take Colson and bring him to safety while the two of us make our way back to the front. Assuming Cara hasn't done anything stupid up to this point, Jei, Stefan, Dean, and I will slowly surround the area before making our attack." Everett lets out a long breath while rubbing his hands down his face.

"Listen, this whole plan sounds smooth. It sounds like an easy in and out operation, but don't underestimate the power of this family. The power of Cara and Cormick. These two have been the head of this organization since Shem fell ill. They are dirty and crooked in every way a mob can be. They won't play fair, so don't fall for any of her bullshit. Anything that comes from their mouths is a lie and no one's life is above their own. You got that?" Dean barks out at the group. I remain still as Dean's attention turns towards me. "No matter what she says to you, Sloan, she wants nothing more than to kill you. She doesn't want you as a sister, a family member, a partner. She wants you dead. Don't fall for any of her tricks." I nod, assuring him I too want nothing more than to end her life.

"Right, you'll move out in ten," Stix says to the group. The guys do one last check through of their weapons while Everett and Dean come to face me. Before either of them can say a word, I speak first.

"I got this; I promise. You both just make sure you get Colson." They both step closer into me, their large frames towering over me, making me feel extra small.

"We know you got this, baby girl. I have no doubts." Everett leans in, cupping my face with his hand before pulling me into his chest and kissing the top of my head for a long moment. Wrapping my arms around him, I squeeze tight, my nerves finally igniting in my stomach at the idea that something could go wrong. What if one of them gets hurt again? What if Cara and Cormick know this is all a scam?

"Don't do that," Everett interrupts my thoughts, pulling me from his chest to peer down at me.

"Do what?"

"Get the negative thoughts out of your head. Do what we came here to do, focus on the task at hand, and execute the plan. Don't allow any other thoughts to invade that pretty little head of yours." I inhale a deep breath, shaking my head once as if it will eliminate the negativity quickly filling my head.

"This is who you're meant to be, love. Show the world who the fuck you are." Giving me one last kiss, he steps away from me, Dean quickly taking up the spot Everett once occupied. He grabs me by the shoulders, holding me firm while his steel-gray eyes lock on my face.

"Do not, under any circumstance, put yourself in a situation to save one of us if things go south. You are not to sacrifice yourself for any of us. You understand me?" His voice is cold and stern as he holds my shoulders tight. "You are to live, Sloan. You promise me that." I look away from his glare, the heat of his eyes is too much for me. "Look at me. You promise me right now, baby girl, or so help me..." He shakes me just slightly, his darkness creeping up from the depths of his core. He's scared, which makes him dangerous in every way a man can be.

"Dean, I love you so much. Know that you, Everett, and Colson have my whole heart and always will. I will follow through with the plan. You'll get Colson and we all go home safely." I can't make a promise I'm not sure I can keep. I would do anything for my guys as they have for me. Promising I won't do anything stupid would be a lie. If push comes to shove, I will do anything to make sure they stay alive. I'm not afraid to die. Hell, in the past I wished for death, but for one of them to die—I can't relive the feelings of losing one of them again. I would rather die myself than live with the loss of them.

Dean lets go of my shoulders, his hands quickly grabbing my hips and lifting me off the ground as he pulls me into his chest. My legs instinctively wrap around his waist, bear hugging him with all my strength. Large arms wrap around my back, holding me close as he rests his face in the crook of my neck.

"I love you, Sloan. So, fucking much."

"I love you too, Dean. Go get our boy." Setting me down gently, he leans in and kisses me softly, his lips gentle and warm as he presses his to mine.

"Right, you lot. Game on." Stix claps his hands together, and I watch as my guys slowly walk away into the darkness of uncertainty. My gut twists in a knot as their figures fade away into the night.

"We got this, little one. Now, let's go fuck some shit up, shall we?" Arno says from behind me as I take in one last deep breath before the veil of revenge falls over me.

"We got this, big man. Let's taste this sweet revenge."

Arno and I make our way to the decoy car we had Stix stash here prior to our arrival. It's an old beat-up BMW he was able to pick up off the streets a few days ago. Before entering the car, Arno zip ties my hands behind my back as discussed. Along with a piece of duct tape over my mouth, and to top off the whole look, a burlap sack to cover my face. Helping me into the front seat, Arno leans over to buckle me in. He smells like timber and bourbon. I inhale his scent, allowing it to fill me with a sense of calm, knowing he'll be with me this whole time.

"Are you sniffing me, little one? No worries, there will be plenty of time for you to hit on me later." He lets out a deep chuckle, knowing I can't respond to his comment due to the duct tape securing my mouth shut. I let out a small huff at his comment. Leave it to Arno to lighten a situation of this magnitude.

The passenger door closes beside me, and a moment later I hear Arno entering the driver's seat. Turning the key in the ignition, the engine comes to life, and we begin driving to the main road. The car is silent, both of us completely engulfed in the roles we are about to play. The decoy and the delivery boy. Arno needs to convince Cara and Cormick he utterly despises Everett, Dean, and Colson so much, that he's willing to hand deliver their most precious thing to their mortal enemy. That's the level of hatred that I hope Arno can portray in hopes of not giving up our true intentions.

"Here we go, little one, time to shine." The car comes to a steady stop, his window rolling down as a gust of cold air fills the cab, making me shiver.

"Who de fuck are ye?" one of the security guards barks out, his Irish accent coming out thick.

"I'm about to be your most valuable player, mate. I have someone here I'm sure the boss is dying to see," Arno casually spits out, while pushing my head to the side.

"That would be?"

"This, my friend, is the granddaughter of Mr. Wallace himself. I hear she's been the talk of the town lately. I figured with some negotiation, we could make a deal, a trade perhaps." Arno's voice is smooth and calculated, every bit of a master manipulator, and I thank God at this moment that he's on our side.

"Ight you, let me see 'er face first." With that, Arno grabs the sack over my head, yanking it up and over my head, making a mess of my long blond hair that is now slapped across my face.

"Here, love, let them see your pretty face." Arno's hands sweep over my face, exposing my duct taped face to the guards. The moment they see my face, an audible gasp escapes one of their mouths.

"Shamus, radio up to de house, tell 'em Sloan is 'ere." My name on his lips gives me goosebumps. Does everyone know who I am?

"Good man," Arno retorts.

"Follow de road up. Stay on the path until ye get to the front. Someone will be there waitin' for ya." Holy shit, it's working. They just let us in, no questions asked. Desperate move if you ask me. I hear Arno roll up his window.

"Too easy, little one, too fucking easy." He shakes his head as he accelerates the car, the driveway lined with massive trees on either side caging us in. It doesn't take long before we round the driveway, pulling up to the massive compound. The guards were right, five men in dark clothing are lined up, each holding AKs that are slung low over their chests.

Stopping the car and shutting off the ignition, Arno exits the car, rounding the back and coming up to the passenger side door. However, he doesn't open it right away, instead he leans his back up against the frame. His giant frame makes the car lean a bit to the side.

"Hello, you lot. I'm here for Cara and Cormick. I have someone they desire, but before I give her up so easily, I'd like to discuss some things first." The men lining the driveway don't say a word. Rather, they remain still, holding their position as if their only job is to look scary. A moment passes and I see Arno fiddling with his fingernails on one hand, looking bored while waiting for someone to speak.

"I have all day." Arno's deep voice breaks the silence once again as he remains leaned up against the car. I adjust myself in my seat, the zip ties biting into my skin.

"Right, I guess I'll be leaving then. I've got more important things to do besides having a staring contest with a bunch of fucking gorillas." Pushing off the car, he takes a step before someone interrupts him.

"What makes ye think ye 'ave somethin' I want?" A cool female voice has the hair on my neck standing on end. Looking out the window, I see a small, slender woman emerge from the cover of her men. Her pin-straight red hair hangs to her waist, her piercing blue eyes visible even in the night. She stands in front of one of her henchmen, her slick black pants and tight black long-sleeve hugging her body as she crosses her arms in front of her.

"Cara, I assume?" Arno bites out, his hands finding his jean pockets before standing tall and rolling his shoulders back, making him look even bigger than the line of men behind her.

"That depends. Who are ye?" Her eyes remain locked on Arno, her gaze not once faltering or wandering.

"You and I have something in common, my dear. We both have a common enemy, you see. A group of men who, since I've been young, have been an annoying thorn in my side. When I heard one of them was killed recently, I became elated. I wanted to know more. I heard through the grapevine that you were looking for someone. Someone that could possibly alter the course of your future." Arno pauses a moment, allowing Cara to absorb his words.

"I guess I've been makin' a lot of noise 'round 'ere. Shame on me."

"You're right, noise travels fast. With one of the problems gone, I figured I'd give you exactly what you want, knowing this will destroy the last two remaining thorns in my side. However, the moment they know their little kitten is gone, you'll be the first person they come looking for. A double-edged sword, if you will. Except now you have a warning. I give you their precious little bitch, and when they come looking for her—and I assure you, they will—you'll have the warning and the manpower to take care of the last two." I swallow the lump building in the back of my throat. Arno should be a fucking actor with how well he is playing the part.

No one speaks for what feels like an eternity. Looking at Cara's profile, she looks pensive, deep in thought at the idea of someone delivering her the person she wants most. Finally, her eyes land on mine, my spine going ramrod straight as a single eyebrow lifts on her delicate face.

"What do you say, my dear?"

Cara continues to stare at me. I stare back, not wanting to be the first to break eye contact. Glancing back to Arno, she gives him a crooked smile.

"Let me see her."

CHAPTER 31

EVERETT

The pain that sparks in my stomach the moment I step away from her is unbearable. It's a hurricane of destruction tearing my insides apart as I step further and further away. *Fuck, get it together, Everett. Focus on what you have to do.*

Dean and I wait for the call from Stone and Cain that will tell us they've started the loop video on the security cameras. It doesn't take long before Stone's voice comes through my earpiece telling us it's safe to proceed. That means she did it. She and Arno should now be making their way up the driveway to the house.

"Fuck, let's go, we don't have much time," I whisper over my shoulder to Dean as we both take off towards the small stone building. A building we're both all too familiar with. Making it to the side of the building, we press our bodies against the cold, wet stones and inch our way along the side, hyperaware of any movement or sounds from lurking guards. It's quiet, only the sounds of the leaves blowing in the wind fill the air. Rounding the corner, I freeze when I see movement coming from the door of the building. A guard exits the room, closing and locking the door behind him and taking off towards the front of the compound.

"The call was just sent through the radio. All men are headed towards the front of the compound. That means you don't have much time," Stone whispers to us through our earpieces.

"Shit, let's go, mate. The longer we take, the longer they'll need to stall," Dean whispers from behind me before he takes off towards the door. He makes quick work of the door, placing a small explosive on the door handle. After securing the explosive, he looks at me, giving me a slight nod before we both turn our faces away. The small bomb detonates with a muffled boom—not loud enough to raise concern.

The door handle instantly crumbles, the door swinging open as we both rush into the small room, our guns at the ready in case any other guards are inside. To our surprise, it's empty. The only audible noise is our heavy breathing as we scan the room for the trapdoor. The air in this building is damp and smells of mold, just how I remembered it.

"There, in the corner." Dean spots the door, and we rush towards it. Grabbing the handle, he lifts the weight of the door with ease. He props the door against the stone wall, and we both peer down inside. Wooden stairs lead into the darkness of the tunnels. We waste no more time; Dean enters the cramped entrance and takes the steps slowly so as not to fall. Following close behind him, I tap his shoulder once, reminding him there's supposed to be a guard, someone close to guard the room Colson occupies. He doesn't answer me, just nods his head once in understanding.

Reaching the bottom of the stairs, my boots meet the dirt ground, the tunnel only leading one way. The ground is illuminated by tiny lights that line the length of the tunnel all the way to the first turn. Dean and I stand side by side, guns raised as we silently make our way down the tunnel. The further into the tunnel we go, the more the air smells of earth and soil. There is a slight decline as we walk, letting me know we are walking further and further into the earth itself. Stopping before he makes it to the first corner, Dean leans his back against the stone wall, and I do the same. Carefully, he peers around the corner, just barely able to see anything, so as not to alert anyone to our presence. Turning to face me, he raises his hand to me, lifting one finger. I nod, grabbing the silencer out of my back pocket and twisting it on the barrel of my pistol. Switching positions, I stand in front of Dean before peering around the corner. I raise my pistol and take the shot. One shot and he's down.

"Right, let's go. Time is running out." Dean rushes from behind me, heading straight for the door. He twists the knob, but it's locked. I kneel down beside the now very dead guard and fish through his pockets to find a key. Reaching into his back pocket, I smile.

"Bingo." I yank out the key and toss it to Dean, who makes quick work of the lock. Before opening the door, we prepare ourselves. Whatever's beyond this door, good or bad, we need to keep our heads on straight. Sloan is quite literally in the lion's den, so whatever state we find Colson in, we have to hold it together, get him to safety, and get back to our girl. I watch as Dean's hand reaches for the handle, and I notice a slight tremor he's trying to hide. This is our brother. Our brother who's been gone for six months and until recently, we thought was dead. A tsunami of emotions washes over my entire body, from my head to my now damp feet. My chest is constricting, and I fear we've waited too long.

Without any more hesitation, Dean slowly turns the knob. The door creaks open slowly as our eyes are met with harsh lighting. It takes a moment and several blinks to get our eyes to adjust to the fluorescent lighting that hangs from the ceiling. The room is small, no bigger than a walk-in closet. Nothing occupies the room except for a single chair. A chair that's occupied by someone whose face is covered with a black sack.

Examining the man, I notice his legs are secured to large metal hooks that've been cemented into the ground. His arms are extended over his head and tied together so tightly with rope, streams of blood have dried down his forearms. He's shirtless, and a number of lacerations, new and old, cover every inch of his chest. I can't tell which ones are old and which ones are fresh because of the amount of dried blood that covers his torso. He isn't wearing socks or shoes. The only article of clothing is a tattered pair of sweats that look three sizes too large from the way they're hanging off his hips. Looking down at his feet, I notice all but two toenails have been removed, each toe is swollen and some leak puss due to obvious infection.

"For fuck's sake," Dean whispers to himself. He takes two large strides towards the man, grabbing the sack that's placed over his head and slowly pulls it free. Long blond hair covers the man's face; however, the man remains still. Rushing over, I wipe the golden locks free from his face and fall to my knees.

"Co-Colson."

CHAPTER 32

SLOAN

Arno turns to face me, and before grabbing the door handle, he shoots me a wink that I hope nobody saw. The car door creaks as he opens it, the sound eerie as it echoes through the night air. I remain still, focusing on breathing one breath at a time. Inhale. Exhale. Inhale. Exhale.

You can do this, Sloan.

Arno leans into the car with me, grabbing the seatbelt and clicking the strap free as it retracts back into the side of the car. He then grabs each one of my legs, swinging them out of the car before grabbing my upper arm and pulling me to my feet. I stumble as Arno leads me forward, playing the part of the captive in hopes she's buying my acting. I look up and down the line of men, landing on Cara, and think to myself. *Where is Cormick?*

"She's quite lovely, aye boys," Cara calls out loud

enough for all her men to hear. No one answers her. Perfectly trained dogs all obeying her every word. They don't look stupid enough to disagree with anything she says.

As she steps towards me, I notice a small shift in Arno. He positions himself slightly in front of me, blocking me from Cara, but not entirely.

"Not so fast, my dear. You haven't agreed to my deal just yet. I give her to you as long as you promise to take care of the other two pains in my arses. Have we reached an agreement?" His tone is firm as he peers down at Cara's small stature. She looks up to him, giving him the most devilish grin I'd ever seen.

"Me question is, why can't ye take care of those bastards ye'self?" She cocks her head to the side, her eyes forming two slits as she questions. However, Arno doesn't falter. He steps in closer to her so they're mere millimeters from being chest to chest, each one holding their ground. The guards behind her shift uneasily until she raises a hand from over her shoulder, stopping them from intervening.

"Because, my dear, it'll look bad on my part if I kill them, being their coworker and all." He pauses a moment before continuing, licking his lips in the most seductive way. I don't miss the slight bob in her throat as she swallows. He's getting to her, that much is certain. "With this plan, it looks like they merely got into a bad business deal, you know, trying to save their pussy and letting their hearts destroy them. A word of advice"—he leans in close to her face, his lips right at her ear—"never let pussy and dick get in the way of business. It never ends well."

Closing her eyes for a moment too long, she takes a step back, craning her neck to look up at Arno, who is smirking down at her in a victorious smile. Arno's playing her at her own game; sex and lust are the most distracting conversation makers. Knowing we have to stall as long as possible, Arno turned on his charm, and fuck, if he hasn't roped her right into his grasp.

Cara places her hand on his chest, pressing just slightly to put some distance between the two of them. She lets out a small huff, rolling her eyes at his charm and turning her back to him.

"Ye say ye work wit dem? What has ye so full of hatred towards dem? They are quite the lookers, if I say so me self." She turns back to face Arno, her hands now planted on her hips. Her long red hair blowing with the slight breeze. I swallow hard, a nervous pit building in the back of my throat at the thought that she may be catching on to our plan. I look to my side at Arno, who doesn't seem the slightest bit fazed by her question. He leans his back against the car, folding his arms across his chest.

"If you must know, I'm fed up with being second best. I'm sure you can relate to that feeling. Am I right?" The scowl that crossed Cara's face shows Arno just hit a nerve. "Anyway, those fuckers have been at the top for too long, and I feel like the company needs a new golden boy, a fresh new face to be called the best, and I am happy to fill those shoes."

I look from Arno to Cara. Their eyes remained locked on one another. Fear bubbles in my chest, and without a second thought, I turn to run. I've been too calm this whole time and feel like a fake escape may be the answer. Arno's arm wraps around the back of my neck, yanking me back to his chest.

"Now, now, little one, let's not do anything stupid shall we?" His breath is warm on the side of my face as he holds me tight, the warmth of his chest making me melt into his frame. A chuckle has me looking at Cara, who is now clapping her hands mockingly.

"Stupid girl, ye think runnin' will get ye anywhere? Look 'round at where ye are. Ye stupid for thinkin' you could escape." She makes her way over to me. Arno's grip on me tightens, ensuring I'm safe with him. However, without warning, Cara raises her hand to me, slapping the side of my face so hard my head snaps to the side. A low growl vibrates in Arno's chest, anger heating his skin.

"Fine," Cara finally declares. "Me men will take 'er from here, and I assure ye we'll take care of them fuckers when dey arrive." She reaches up and grabs my upper arm, yanking me free of Arno's grasp. Realization hits me like a freight train.

In Arno's last-ditch effort to stall this conversation further, he blurts out, "What's say you and I continue getting to know each other in a more private location? How's that sound, sweetheart?"

Cara pushes me towards her men, two large arms wrap around my shoulders holding me immobile. Sauntering up to Arno, he flicks his gaze from me to her as she slowly approaches him, her hands resting on his chest.

"I hate to break it to ye, big boy, but I'm spoken for," Cara's seductive voice whispers loud enough for the rest of us to hear. Reaching up to her face, Arno brushes a loose strand of her hair behind her ear. The way Cara's back relaxes at his touch shows me his technique is working.

"That she is spoken for." A deep voice makes me jump as someone emerges from the shadows behind me. "Long time no see, Arno." I can't see who's talking. The guard's hold on me is so restricting, it's almost hard to breathe.

Lifting up on her tiptoes, Cara kisses the side of Arno's cheek before backing away from him and facing me.

"Arno. Sloan. I'd like for ye to meet Callum. However, I think ye've all met before."

My blood runs cold, my wide eyes meeting Arno's, who's looking over the top of my head with a look that could kill.

"Arno, mate, you don't look too happy to see me. It's been a long time."

I try to hide the slight tremble in my knees as I remain still, allowing the guard's arm to hold me upright. I focus on my breathing, trying to remain calm as footsteps come up from behind. I'm still staring at Arno, his brows furrowed tightly, his fore-head creases above his dark eyes.

I can see him in my peripherals, his tall stature coming into my line of sight as he invades the space in front of me. Looking up, I see him, his dark eyes fixated on my face as his fingers catch beneath my chin, tilting my head further towards his face.

"Hello, love. Miss me?"

CHAPTER 33

DEAN

Colson's body slumps forward, the rope secured to his wrists the only thing keeping him upright. Everett's pained voice fills the small room.

"Co-Colson?" I wrap my arms around his torso, gently so as not to hurt him anymore than he already is. Leaning him back in the chair, his head falls back, a deep purple and blue bruise spreads across his neck. I have to swallow to keep the bile from rising in my throat any further. Anger, pain, and sadness are swirling within me at the sight of my brother bruised, beaten, tortured, and emaciated to a state I've never seen before—and I've seen some fucked-up shit.

I make quick work of the ropes securing his wrists, while Everett does the same with the ropes around his ankles.

"Hold on, mate, we're here. Everett and I are here." My voice cracks, guilt rearing its ugly face as I carefully lower each of his arms as I untie them. As soon as I free his arms, I gently place two fingers on his throat to make sure he's alive. It takes a moment, but I can feel the faintest pulse, and I let out a breath of relief.

"He's alive," I manage to whisper.

"Fucking barely, look at him," Everett barks, his anger mixed with guilt evident in his voice. "Come on, we need to get him to Stone and Cain immediately." I nod to Everett, the pair of us grabbing an arm and wrapping them around our shoulders.

"On the count of three. One. Two. Three." Lifting Colson's limp body, we carefully make our way back to the door. I kick the dead guard as hard as I can, moving his body out of the way. As we carry Colson down the tunnel, he lets out a pained moan as we round the corner and head towards the stairs.

"You're alright, mate, we've got you," Everett groans. Colson is by far the lightest among the three of us, but when it comes to deadweight, anything feels heavy. Reaching the stairs, I shift Colson's weight to Everett so I can get ahead of him. We take our time, taking one step at a time until we finally reach the top. I radio into Stone and Cain informing them we have Colson and we're bringing him out now.

Exiting the stone building, we head to the drop location where we hand off Colson to the guys.

"For fuck's sake, is he alive?" Stone asks, as we

help get Colson in the back of the suburban where Cain is waiting with medical supplies.

"Yes, he's fucking alive. Just clean him up the best you can and get him some water!" I bellow to Stone. He doesn't respond, just hops in the back with Cain and begins their assessment of Colson.

"Come on, we don't have much time," I say to Everett, as the pair of us jog back around the compound. Silently, we make it to the stone building once again. Checking our surroundings, we creep around the building. Our plan is to come up from behind, bringing the element of surprise. I look at Everett silently mouthing, "On the count of three." —I raise my fingers—"one, two, three."

The moment we round the corner, we stop dead in our tracks.

"Hello, brother, you miss me?" The smirk on Callum's face is my undoing, and I see red. I ram my shoulder directly into his gut, throwing him onto his back with a thud. He lets out a groan as the wind gets knocked out of him. Rising up, I swing my fist over and over again connecting with his face; blood soon covers my knuckles.

A sharp jab to my ribs bends me over. I suck in a breath as the sharp pain feels like a knife to my side. Callum shoves me from his chest, his fist cracking against my jaw as I fall back to the wet grass. Everett is right there, wrapping his bicep around his brother's neck and pulling him to his feet. I shoot to my feet, tightening my fists as I deliver blow after blow to Callum's stomach. Low groans escaping his throat as he continues to fight Everett's grip on his neck. Just when Callum's body begins to slowly slump over from lack of oxygen, I'm thrown to the grass once more. I'm crushed by a force I didn't see coming. The recognizable sound of metal clicking above me has me stilling as I turn to look up at a man who is pointing a gun directly at my temple.

"Didn't I kill you already, mate?" His voice is nails on a chalkboard, as I slowly rise to my feet, his gun never once leaving my head.

"Van. I see you're still playing the role of someone's bitch. As always," I cough out as I try to catch my breath.

"Nah, mate, you see that's where you're wrong. I've never been anyone's bitch. I'm a key player here. Look who's got the gun." He laughs as he looks at me down his barrel.

"You really think you're the only one with a gun? You really are stupider than you look, mate." Everett draws Van's attention from me as he holds a gun to Callum's head. His brother continuing to struggle beneath his hold.

"Put the gun down, Van, and maybe I won't kill your bestie here." Callum chuckles to himself, the maniacal sound making me tense.

"Nah, I think not. You lower yours and we'll all have a nice conversation as to why the hell you're both here." The moment Van has his full attention on Everett, I make my move. Grabbing his gun with both hands, I twist his wrist to the side, cracking his wrist and forcing him to release his weapon. I don't hesitate. I whip the gun against Van's nose, the impact instantly causing blood to shoot from his nostrils. He lets out a pained cry, his body hitting his knees as he cups his face in his hands. I hit him again. The butt of his gun connects with his temple, and he slumps to the ground, instantly falling unconscious.

"Too easy," I say under my breath before looking back up to Callum, who's now glaring daggers at me. Holding Van's gun in my hand, I release the full clip, as well as the bullet in the chamber, and quickly disassemble his gun and toss it to the wood line before retrieving my own. Walking over to my gun that I dropped to the ground when tackling Callum, I wipe off the wet grass and begin twisting on my silencer. Walking over to Callum and Everett, I look between the two.

"You know, if you weren't such a psychotic piece of fucking shit that doesn't even deserve to be the mud on my boots, the organization could've really used a twin duo." I raise my gun to Cal's forehead, pressing the silencer painfully hard against his forehead, when Everett stops me.

"Wait, Dean, I have an idea." The look on Everett's face is full of sin. Whatever idea he has swimming in his head has my curiosity spiked. Everett squeezes Callum's throat harder, his body thrashing beneath his hold until he slowly goes limp and falls to the ground.

"Let's play them at their own game even further," he whispers to me; he begins undressing and I catch his hint. I quickly remove Cal's clothes, tossing Everett his shirt and then his jeans. Dressing as quickly as possible, Everett teases his hair with his fingers, portraying his identical but untidied brother's hair.

"How do I look?" he asks me with a devious smile pulling at his lips. I chuckle at his question.

"You look like one of the King twins, if I'm being honest. Couldn't tell you two apart if I hadn't grown up with you two bastards." We both let out a laugh as we peer down at Callum's unconscious body splayed across the wet ground. Everett lifts his gun from his side and fires off two shots, one hitting Callum in the head and one to his chest.

"I've been wanting to do that for years. Now there's only one Everett King." I clap Everett on his shoulder, a sense of relief washing over his face.

"Let's finish this," Everett says. Before we leave, I point my gun at Van, shooting him twice in the head.

"That's for our girl and the warehouse. See you in hell." I spit on his body before turning on my heel and making my way around the back of the house.

Time to get our girl and head home.

CHAPTER 34

SLOAN

Callum's fingers are gentle on my chin. His eyebrows pinch together as his plump lips slowly pull into a smile. I study his face; fuck, he looks just like Everett. Their sharp jawline, the constant five o'clock shadow that's impeccably maintained, and those eyes. Those deep emerald-green eyes that can see directly through my soul and straight to my heart.

"The way you're breathing tells me you most certainly missed me." His thumb brushes my cheek, and I pull my face from his grasp before he can see me blush.

"Oh, don't be like that, love. You and I both know if we weren't interrupted that night, we would have had so much fun together." Fingers grab the edge of the duct tape on my face and rip it free. Wincing at the pain, I lick my dry lips before spitting at Callum's feet.

"Now, love, is that how a lady should act?" He tisks with his tongue.

"So, Cal, what've you been up to these past few years? Haven't heard from you. Hell, you don't call, don't write. I was starting to think you may have died." Arno pulls Cal's attention away from me, his body turning slowly to face him.

"You know, just dabbling in this and that, nothing too exciting if I'm being honest. Living my life, the way I should be, not taking orders from others who can't do their own dirty work." Cal puts his hands in his pockets, his posture ever so relaxed as he talks to Arno as if he's a longtime friend.

"For fuck's sake, this isn't a school reunion. Cal, say goodbye to ye friend, we have business to 'andle here!" Cara barks to the group. I almost forgot she was here. Cal's presence is so dominating, he calls all the attention.

"Right, sorry, my dear, you're right." Cal turns his attention to Cara, who's standing tall with her hands on her hips and her once delicate face twisted in anger.

"Well, mate, it was a pleasure to see you. We should catch up some time," Arno says, taking a step closer to Cara. Grabbing her hand, he lifts it to his mouth, kissing the top sweetly before giving her a wink.

"Remember our deal, love. It was a pleasure doing business with you." She blushes at his compliment, dropping her hand to her side as he releases her.

"Right, Cara, my love, would you mind fetching Cormick so we can have a little family reunion?" Cal calls to her. Silence falls upon the group. Cara's eyes narrow into slits as her head tilts to the side at Cal's request. Clearing her throat, she straightens her posture, adjusting her blouse before smoothing it down with her hands.

Just then, Cara pulls her gun from her holster and points it directly at Cal's head. Following suit, the guards do the same. Each one pointing their rifles at Cal, who doesn't flinch in the slightest. Arno shifts on his feet with unease as he looks at me with a hardening expression.

"It's funny, sweetheart, you want me to go fetch Cormick when ye were the one to end his life almost seven months ago." Cara's seething, her once pale skin now bright red with rage. Cal takes a step back towards me, his body now positioned between me and the guards, as if he's protecting me. He takes a few more steps back, shielding me from anyone's line of fire.

"Silly me, must have slipped my mind," Cal says, raising his hands in surrender. Turning his head to the side, he whispers, "Now." The guards' bodies hit the ground simultaneously, the sound of each one hitting the stone path making me grin internally. Blood slowly pools around their bodies; each one having been shot. Cara lets out a scream of rage, her gun still pointed at Cal as her gaze roams over her now lifeless guards.

"If you were smart, you'd see you are now painfully outnumbered." Arno's voice is cold as death as he now has his gun pointed at the side of Cara's head. "I suggest lowering your weapon if you don't want to end up like your boys over there." She does as he says, slowly lowering her gun to her side before dropping it to the ground with a thud.

"Ye think you've won. Ye think Shem isn't goin' to be mad when he finds out Sloan is the reason his only grandson is dead." This psychotic bitch really thinks she's going to put his death on me. She's more delusional than I was giving her credit for.

"Turn around, love," Cal, or rather Everett, says as he pulls his knife from his pocket, freeing my hands. I rub my wrists as I slowly step closer to Cara, Everett following close behind.

"Ye think your dogs can protect ye, foolish little girl?" she says, her gaze darting from Everett and me.

"I've got me own twin too, darlin'," she laughs out.

"Oh, you mean this twin?" Dean's voice draws my attention to the side of the house. My smile is now impossible to hide as I watch Cara begin to crumble right in front of my eyes. It's fucking beautiful. Dean's large frame emerges along with a slumped over Cal, who he's dragging by his arm through the wet grass. "Yeah, he wasn't being a very good boy. We had to put him down. Can never trust a dog that bites, you know what I mean?" He drops Cal's limp and very dead body before making his way over to stand beside me.

"Like I said, this isn't over," she growls out, her body shaking with anger as a lone tear falls from her eye, leaving a wet streak down her cheek at the sight of Cal's body.

"Oh, I think dis is all very much over wit, Cara." Arno redirects his gun to an older gentleman I didn't see walking slowly towards the five of us. Walking behind him are two middle-aged men in black suits, looking unfazed at the chaos they just entered.

"Lower ye gun boy, I'm no threat to ye." The men in suits grab Cara by her arms and pull her behind the older man, who is now staring directly at me.

"Ye must be, Sloan. I've been lookin' for ye. I'm Shem, your grandfather."

I can't help the gasp that leaves my lips at the sight of my grandfather standing in front of me. He looks just the same as he did that day he came looking for me as a little girl. He takes another step towards me. Everett and Dean stand in front of me, protecting me with their bodies.

"Listen boys, I told ye I'm not goin' to hurt her. I want to apologize."

Apologize...I didn't see that coming.

"Shem, she can't be trusted, she killed—" Cara's words are cut off mid-cry.

"I suggest ye shut ye mouth." Shem pulls a gun from behind his back, pointing it directly at Cara's face. She gasps in surprise, her eyes going wide in fear. He takes a step closer to her, his expression hardening.

"Did ye think killin' off ye siblings would be the answer to inheriting me fortune?" he shouts down at her. He's not tall by any means, not nearly as tall as Everett or Dean, but he is taller than Cara, who is now hunched low as he scolds her like a small puppy. "Did ye think I wouldn't find out? Shame on ye, girl, shame on ye."

"Shem, I'm sorry. Listen, ye have to believe me, she is a threat!" A loud noise pierces the air, my body flinching at the bang that reverberates through the night. Smoke plums from the end of my gun, and a lifeless Cara lies on the ground, her eyes still wide as blood leaks from the gaping hole in her forehead. My jaw hangs low—shock and disbelief clouding my brain. I killed Cara.

With an outstretched arm, I continue pointing my gun in the direction of Cara as Dean places his hand over the top of the barrel. Slowly lowering the gun to the floor, he wraps his fingers around mine and takes the gun from my grasp. Shem turns to face me with an unreadable expression on his face. His hands find his suit jacket where he buries his hands in deep. His breathing is short and erratic, a cough slipping from his lips between every breath.

"Can't say she didn't 'ave that comin'." He's not fazed in the slightest that I killed his granddaughter in cold blood. I expect him, or even his men, to rush me, but everyone remains where they stand. This is the life I live now, where murder is just another day at the office.

"As ye can see, I'm a very sick man. Not much longer for me, I reckon." Pulling out a white cloth, he covers his mouth and coughs several coughs, choking and spitting as he does. I wince at the wet noises he creates. Pulling the cloth from his mouth, I see bright red smears, blood coming up with each cough he delivers. I lick my lips, my throat suddenly going dry.

"I'm sorry we had to meet under these circumstances. I hoped I'd meet ye before I took me last breath. I wanted to give ye somethin'." Shem extends his hand towards one of his men, who hands him a manilla envelope. He takes a step closer to me, but Dean stands in front of me as Shem hands him the envelope.

"Don't open it now. It's for when I die, which shouldn't be too much longer." He takes a deep breath before continuing, the act looking painful as he winces with the rise and fall of his chest. "I apologize for dis cruel life ye've lived so far. I tried getting custody of ye when ye was a wee lass, but ye father wouldn't allow dat. When I came lookin' for ye, I saw the conditions ye were in, and I knew I needed to intervene. However, America has a way of doin' things that make it difficult, even when it's apparent a child is suffering. I'm just sorry I couldn't save ye." He coughs more into his cloth, more blood bubbling from his throat.

One of his men rests his hand on his shoulder before whispering at his side.

"Talkin' makes it worse sir, I suggest—" Shem cuts him off, raising his hand to silence him.

"I'm dead already." Shem wipes his mouth once again before straightening his back and continuing. "I want ye to know dis business, dis life is not somethin' I want for me grandkids. As ye can see, money and power can turn the best of people into monsters." He waves his hand at Cara's body, a perfect example of what could happen when the promise of such wealth goes to your head. "I don't want dis business for ye. I want ye to live—live a life with these boys who clearly love you in a way ye deserve. Stay with them. Live happily, erase the horrors of ye past, and build the life ye want. Ye are strong, Sloan, that much is certain. It's clear ye've followed a path worth continuing on. I admire ye will to live, sweetheart. I'm sorry for me son, and the childhood he robbed from ye. I hope what's in that envelope will show ye how much I care for ye, even though this is our first meeting and, quite possibly our last."

Shem coughs some more, his white cloth now completely saturated in blood as my eyes begin to sting with fresh tears. I don't know this man. I never thought I'd see him again after he came looking for me all those years ago. Looking at him now—aged, sick, and rapidly deteriorating in front of me—I pity him. He wanted what I've wanted my whole life—a family. Not only have I been robbed of a family, he has too. His son—my father—Cara, and Cormick had all turned into the very monsters he speaks about. I watch him as he continues to cough and gasp for air when his knees start to tremble. I push past Everett and Dean, rushing towards Shem to catch him as he slowly falls to the ground.

Wrapping my arms around his chest, I ease his body towards the ground, his weight too much to hold up. We both hit the wet ground, as his body begins to shake as his men cradle his head in their hands.

"Shem," I whisper, my voice shaking as his face stares up at mine. His eyes are a deep blue, not as bright as mine, but more of a deep ocean-blue. Reaching his hand to my face, he cups my face in his large, calloused hand.

"I'm sorry, me child." Tears rush down my cheeks, a sob escaping my lips. "Ye look just like ye grandmother, she would 'ave loved ye." I smile down at him. A broken man I only wish could've been a part of my life even for a moment longer, but he's fading fast. Those deep blue eyes become hazy and distant, but he still stares up at me, a small smile pulling at his lips before his whole body relaxes against me.

Life is cruel, just like love. We're never dealt the hand we wish. It's truly unfair. The one thing in this world I've ever wished for has just died in my arms. Bowing my head, I let it all out. I scream into the darkness of the night. I scream so hard my throat starts to hurt. My tears fall against his body, my sobs are uncontrollable as Dean and Everett kneel down beside me. I don't know how long I cry over Shem's lifeless body, but no one interrupts me. They let me grieve, let me feel, let me say goodbye.

I lower my face to his, kissing his forehead gently. "Goodbye, Shem," I whisper before lifting my head towards his men. Giving me a slight nod, the pair of them grab hold of Shem's arms, hosting him up and carrying him to the front of the house. Arno follows them, opening the door for them and then closing it behind them. Coming to where I'm kneeling on the ground, the three of us stand in unison as I collect myself, wiping my face clean of tears and brushing off my knees.

Footsteps crunch over the gravel behind us. Turning, I see Jei, Stefan, and Cain joining us with their rifles slung over their backs. Just then my heart begins to race as I face Everett and Dean and whisper, "Colson? Is he—?"

"Baby girl, he's alive," Everett says, leaning down and capturing my face in his hands. His forehead rests against mine, and I fully and completely crumble.

CHAPTER 35

SLOAN

We all make our way back to our safe location where the suburban sits. Stone is leaning against the open back hatch, wiping his hands with a cloth before he notices the seven of us approaching. Pushing off the back, he turns to face us, his face neutral and unreadable. My heart is pounding so hard in my chest I can feel it in my ears.

I run towards the SUV. Stone's arm grabs me by the waist, stopping me before I can see inside.

"Listen, he's stable, but we need to get him home as soon as possible. He's lost a lot of blood; he's malnourished, and I'm pretty sure he has an infection from one of his wounds. His fever is high, and we need to act fast." Releasing my waist, I step closer to the back hatch, peering inside. Colson lays wrapped in thick blankets, his head resting on a pillow. An IV is inserted into his arm, providing fluids. My hands go to my mouth with shock and disbelief at the state of his face. His once golden bright face is covered in black, blue, and purple discoloration. Several lacerations and new scars pepper his cheeks, jaw, and forehead. It's worse than I thought.

My eyes become blurry with tears. I'm frozen to the ground. The sound of footsteps coming up behind me has me turning my head.

"Fuck," Arno whispers out, his gaze falling on Colson. A pair of hands rests on my shoulders and I grab them, squeezing them tightly.

"Why don't you crawl in beside him, love? We need to get him to headquarters as soon as possible." Dean's lips are at my ear, his warm breath feathering over my skin. I do as he says. I crawl in beside Colson, being careful not to disturb his IV or wake him. The rest of the guys pile into the suburban, Stix already in the driver's seat as we take off down the gravel road.

He's unrecognizable. Is this really him? A once beautiful face is discolored with deep blues, blacks, and purples covering every available inch of skin. His nose is bent at an odd angle, obviously broken in multiple places. An unfamiliar wound is peeking out from beneath the blanket that's covering his chest. Curiosity gets the best of me and I gently pull down the blanket, exposing a long rectangular wound that looks to be fresh by how red and inflamed it is. I study the wound; skin has been removed with perfect edges, as if a cookie cutter was punctured through his chest and the skin was peeled back.

"It was caused by a tool they use in surgery, little one. When they need to do a skin graft, they basically peel back skin and relocate it to other parts of the body. Think of it as a cheese grater. That's what that's from," Arno informs me from the back seat, his voice pained as he explains the wound to me. He's turned his body, looking over the back of the seat. Tears begin to sting my eyes again as I continue looking down at Colson's still body.

"I have to say, he's a strong motherfucker for making it this long. That's a new level of torture," he adds, his hand resting on my shoulder as fat tears stream down my cheeks.

"Six months, he was tortured for six months, and not once did he give Cara what she wanted," I sniff, trying desperately not to break out in sobs.

"That's called love, baby girl. His love kept him alive, that I'm sure of," Everett whispers to me. He's sitting beside Arno, and I hadn't even realized it. Looking up to him, I see his eyes are holding back tears. His eyes are fixated on Colson, his jaw clenching tight as his eyes roam over his body. Turning his head towards the window, I don't miss the tear that falls down his cheek. As much as it hurts seeing him this way, I can't imagine Everett and Dean's pain seeing their brother in this state. Colson is their brother, their best friend, their family. I may not have blood relatives, but Everett, Dean, and

Colson are my family, my heart, and seeing either one of them hurt is a knife to my own heart.

Gently leaning down, I snuggle my head into the crook of Colson's arm. I never thought in this lifetime I'd be able to do this again. Never thought I'd see this beautiful soul, touch him, feel his warmth, listen to his heart beat. With that, I let out a soft cry. I fall asleep to the sounds of my own cries, exhaustion slowly taking hold of me as I snuggle deeper into Colson's body.

"Baby girl, we're at the plane. Wake up." Dean's soft voice fills my head as I slowly open my eyes. Reaching for Colson's body, I'm met with air. He's gone. Panic floods through my veins. My eyes snapping open as I sit straight up, hitting my head on the roof of the suburban.

"Easy, love, you're safe. I'm here." Dean holds tight to my shoulders, keeping me steady as I search throughout the vehicle. "He's already on the plane. Everything's already loaded up. Time to go home." My eyes adjust to the darkness, and I hurriedly exit the back, looking around to see everyone else congregating at the entrance to the plane. Dean grabs my hand, pulling me close to his side as we make our way to the plane.

"Thanks again, mate. We couldn't have done this without you." Everett's shaking Stix's hand with appreciation.

"Once a Shadow, always a Shadow. All you have to do is call." As we approach, Dean claps Stix's shoulder, squeezing him in thanks. As Dean directs me to the stairs, I stop and turn to face Stix. Without a word, I give him a hug, words feeling like not enough at this moment. His thick arms wrap around my body, his head resting on top of mine.

"Be good, girl. And if these fools get to be too much, you call me and I'll handle them," Stix whispers in my ear, making me smile against his chest. I pull back to look up at his aging face. "Somehow, though, I feel as though you can handle yourself quite well." His finger pokes my nose as he speaks, a gesture I could only imagine a grandfather doing to his granddaughter, and I smile.

"Thank you for everything," I manage to say without bursting into tears. Giving me a smile, he ushers me to the plane.

"Better get a move on. He's going to need medical attention as soon as you land." I give him a nod and turn to board the plane. The cold air blows through my hair as I take a deep breath. It's done, we did it. Colson is alive and we're going home. Reaching my arm back for Dean, he grabs my hand once again and follows me into the plane.

The plane ride feels shorter than before. I'm sitting in between Everett and Dean on the leather sofa towards the rear of the plane. I look to my right and see Everett's eyes are closed, his head leaned back on the sofa and his mouth is slightly open as he softly snores. Turning to my left, Dean has his head propped on his hand, his elbow resting on the sofa's armrest.

Then I look to the back of the plane. Colson is laying on a small cot, his body covered in a blanket as he remains asleep. I smile to myself. The thought of all three of my guys breathing and alive makes my insides feel light. It's a feeling unlike anything I've ever felt. You know when you're underwater and you feel like you can't hold your breath any longer, then suddenly your head breaches the surface? Your lungs fill with air and your chest no longer feels tight— everything just feels peaceful, and you've made it? That's the feeling.

"I'm so fucking happy for you, little one," Arno whispers to me from across the plane. When I look up towards him, he's leaning his arms on his knees, his eyes locked on my face as his head tilts slightly to the side. The corner of my lips lifts to a small smile as I stare back into his dark eyes.

"Why do you say that, big man?" He shifts his body so he's sitting on the edge of his seat. "You've beaten all the odds; you've found your heart. All four pieces are now placed together into a perfect match." He takes a small breath before continuing, "And you got the revenge you deserved." Combing his hair back with his hand, he grabs the back of his hoodie, pulling it above his head. His shirt gets caught under-neath his hoodie, lifting it up as he yanks the fabric from his torso, exposing his ripped abdomen.

Willow.

One word tattooed in delicate handwriting written across his right hip bone has my smile instantly falling. Willow. Colson's diary. My eyes darted to Colson and then back to Arno, who's now looking at me with a confused expression.

"What's that face for?" he asks me, his eyebrows pinching together. There has to be a connection between the two names, right? Willow, who was found by Colson, has to be the same Willow Arno has been searching for all this time? My eyes soften on Arno's face. This man, so full of mystery, transitioning from one of my enemies to my closest friend. Arno has helped me and succeeded in saving my guys, all three of them. I have to find Willow for him. I need to help this broken, determined, devoted man find his heart as he's helped me find mine.

"Nothing," I lie to him. Then I get up from my seat and throw myself onto Arno, hugging him as I squeeze my arms as tight as I can. His arms wrap around my body, lifting me up and sitting me on his knee. "Thank you for helping me, for saving them and making me whole again. I couldn't have done this without you, big guy." The back of my eyes stings again, but I hold them at bay. Arno's chest rises and falls with a deep breath.

"You're welcome, little one." We stay like this for a long moment, embracing one another. In this moment, I promise to myself I will find his Willow; I will do everything in my power to save this man as he's saved me.

CHAPTER 36

COLSON

"Alright, two more, you've got this." Smith's voice sounds like nails on a chalkboard at this point. I extend my right leg two more times as he instructs, and I let out a breath of pain and frustration as the weights clang together. I've been in physical therapy since recovering at the organization under the supervision of our doctors. Once arriving back at headquarters, I was assessed, tested, and scanned for any and everything possible. After many tests, x-rays and imaging it was found I had suffered a femur fracture in two places that had healed awkwardly. Doctors had to go in, re-break the bones and reset them for the bones to heal properly.

Among all the other injuries I endured such as a broken nose, several lacerations sustained from knives, wipes, cattle prongs, surgical instruments, electric drills, and my least favorite the dermatome— or cheese grater. This was one of Cara's favorite tools to use on me. I have six new scars from that fucking tool. Two on my left arm, one on my left pectoral muscle, one on each calf, and the most painful one being on my back. I also suffered from eight broken fingers, a broken wrist, a dislocated jaw, a broken eye socket, and a shattered right foot. Yeah, she did a number on me, that's for sure.

These past months have been nothing but recovery for me, physically and mentally. Smith has been in charge of my physical rehabilitation, while Ms. Janice has been in charge of my mental rehab. If I had to pick, I'd say Janice has the harder job. Since returning home, I've been having intense nightmares that leave me short of breath and drenched in sweat. That's not the worst of it, however. Dean has had to pull me off Sloan more than once, waking me with my hands tightly gripped around her neck. My dreams are so vivid, it's like I can feel Cara's throat beneath my fingers, but every time I'm woken by Dean, it's Sloan's face I see. Her red face as I drain life from her. Just as her eyes begin to roll back, Dean successfully pulls me off her. It was so bad; I began locking myself in my room at night and refusing to have her sleep beside me. I couldn't bear hurting her like I was. What if I killed her by accident? I couldn't live with myself. She begged and pleaded with me to let her sleep in my bed with me. I finally gave in. I let her sleep beside me. However, when she finally does fall asleep, I move her to her room or one of the guys' rooms before locking myself back in my room. As mad as she gets in the morning when she realizes I moved her, she understands my fear.

We've been inseparable since coming home. She's not left my side through this whole recovery. She sits in the corner of the room now, reading her cute little romance book as I struggle through my session with Smith.

"Right, mate, you're doing so well. Much improvement from last week," Smith informs me, extending his hand to help me exit the machine, but I don't take it. "You should be back to feeling like yourself in no time. Till then keep up with the stretches at home and no lifting on your own unless you're with me." Giving me a stern glare, he claps my shoulder before leaving me. I turn to face Sloan. She's so absorbed with her book she doesn't even see me approaching her. Her delicate lips pulled into a small smile as her cheeks start turning a light shade of pink. She's reading a sex scene, of this, I am sure.

"Want to recreate that scene you're reading about? Looks to me like it could be a good one." Slamming the book closed, she lifts her face, her eyes meeting mine. Busted.

"Wh-what are you talking about?" She fumbles through her words. Her cheeks are quickly turning a beautiful shade of pink as I raise an eyebrow at her, awaiting her response.

"Fine, you caught me. Is that what you wanted to hear?" She giggles, standing from her chair and wrapping her arms around my torso, her hair falling down her back as the scent of wild berry and vanilla fills my nostrils. I inhale her scent; I could never get enough of this woman. Her scent, her touch, her presence—I want it all. I never want to let her go or leave her side again. Those six months were by far the longest days and nights of my life. Every day I was away from her, my chest cracked and splintered deeper and deeper.

Looking up from where her head rests on my chest, she smiles up at me.

"What's got you smiling so big?" she asks me, her head tilting slightly to the side. I brush the loose strands of her hair out of her face before answering.

"I'm here, with you. Nothing could be better than this." Bright blue eyes begin to water as her smile widens across her face at me. I hug her a moment longer, not wanting to let her go before she lifts off my chest, wrapping her delicate fingers through mine.

"Come on, Romeo, the guys texted me an hour ago saying dinner was just about ready." Pulling my arm, she leads me from the physical therapy room and down the many halls of the headquarters. Just as we're rounding the corner, she comes to an abrupt halt, causing me to crash into her back. We both practically fall to the floor when faint voices filter through the hall. It's Arno. I'd recognize that man's deep raspy voice even in the afterlife. Sloan is frozen in front of me, her ears perked up and eavesdropping on whomever he's speaking to. I listen in as well, wondering what's got my girl so curious.

"She's alive, mate. I know she is. I won't stop until she's safe. There's an auction tonight at the Fortress and I'm feeling optimistic about this one," Arno says to whoever he's speaking to.

"Listen, mate, I want to find her as much as you do—" The second voice is cut off by Arno, his voice rising as his frustration gets the best of him.

"No, you don't want to find her as much as I do! No one here will ever understand the desperation I feel about finding her. The only other person that has felt the way I'm feeling now is Sloan. The difference between her and I is that she found her happily ever after. I haven't." I look down at Sloan's back, her shoulders rising and falling with deep breaths.

"Actually, we have to do something before we leave today. Come with me." Sloan whirls around, whispering to me as she drags me down the opposite hallway. We're practically running, her hand squeezing mine as she directs me around corner after corner. It isn't until we get to the door she's hunting for that I finally ask, "What are we doing?"

"We're finding Arno's happily ever after."

CHAPTER 37

SLOAN

After Colson and I finished at headquarters, we finally pulled into our driveway. Pressing the garage door button, we wait for the hatch to open fully before he pulls his Audi R8 into his designated bay. He then presses the garage button once again, closing it behind us. We enter the house together, and the smell of garlic fills my nose as I inhale a deep breath, smiling at the delicious scent. We make our way into the kitchen to find Everett and Dean standing around the island laughing and conversing together.

"Fuck yes, you ordered Rocco's!" Colson claps his hands together, racing over to grab a plate and begins piling a mound of spaghetti onto his plate. Since Colson's return, he's slowly begun packing on the much-needed pounds he lost for those six months. Looking at him inhaling the spaghetti, I'd say he's just about back to his normal weight.

Standing at the entrance to the kitchen, I smile to myself. Everett, Dean, and Colson all here, all breathing, and all mine again. My heart has never felt so full in its life. Dean's eyes catch mine, his expression mirroring mine as he loads up a plate and makes his way over to me.

"I know, baby girl. It still doesn't seem real that he's back. We're whole again." He grabs my hand with his free one and leads me to the island, where he pulls out a chair for me. I take my seat as he places the plate down in front of me and pushes my chair in closer.

The four of us eat together as a family, reconnected. Colson's sitting beside me on my right while Everett is standing opposite of us enjoying his own plate and a full glass of red wine. Dean is sitting on the countertop as he usually does, eating four large pieces of parmesan chicken. The man can eat. Then there's me; the girl who was kidnapped, saved, kidnapped again, saved again, kidnapped and tortured, saved, manipulated, heart ripped from her chest, heart reconstructed and put back together. A true horror story turned happily ever after. My life is a revolving door of traumatic events that somehow turned out to be okay in the end.

Looking back on that day, walking home from the café, there is truly nothing I could have done differently to avoid any of this, and seeing at my guys now, I wouldn't have it any other way. I was saved from my previous life in a crazy way. Redirected from one awful path to another that, although it has equally terrifying and traumatic experiences up ahead, it also has love. Love being the human emotion I'd never felt in my entire life, not until three mysterious men swooped in and changed the course of my life forever. I'm a different person now, evolving from a timid, frightened girl who constantly glancing over her shoulder at the idea her parents could show up at any moment, to a woman who is stronger, independent, and able to forge her own future without the fears of others taking from her again.

"What do you say, love, you in?" My head snaps up, and I see all three of my guys are now staring at me.

"In for what?" I ask, giving away that I was zoning out and not paying attention to their conversation. Colson lets out a laugh, stuffing in another large bite of spaghetti.

"Are you in for a little midnight swim with us?" I light up, my heart racing with excitement. Since Colson was taken, I hadn't swum in the pool. The pain of him being gone was too much for me to bear, but now that he's home, my heart longs for a good swim. Then it dawns on me.

"Colson, is it true you can't swim?" Everett practically spits out the sip of wine he was taking as Dean lets out the deepest belly laugh I've ever heard him do. The look Colson gives the guys is telling—it's true, he can't swim. My cheeks pull into a grin as he fumbles over his words.

"What the hell, guys?! Listen, baby, I can swim. I promise." He bellows.

"Are you sure about that?" Dean says between laughs.

"Listen, you fucker, I can swim. I'm just not what you would call a strong swimmer."

"Baby girl, that means he can't fucking swim." Dean looks at me, his eyes watering from laughing so hard. Colson's hazel eyes find mine, his brows furrowed in a playful expression as he jumps from his seat and positions himself in front of me. Before I can escape his grasp, he hoists me over his shoulder, smacking my ass, and turns to the sliding glass doors.

"I'll show you assholes I can swim," Colson says, grabbing the door and sliding it open. Looking up, I see Everett and Dean are quickly removing their shirts and then their pants, leaving them in nothing but their boxers. They follow after us, racing ahead of one another to reach the door first. Just then I'm weightless, the world tilting on its axis before I'm swallowed by the gravitational pull of the pool's surface.

Silence. Silence fills my ears as the water surrounds every inch of me, the feeling of being in perfect harmony exploding in my chest. Water has a way of making you feel small—nothing more than a speck of matter floating in its hold. It's addicting and mesmerizing all at once. The perfect drug that I've been missing. What I've been craving but too scared to feel the pain of the memories created within its hold. Until now.

Opening my eyes, he's right there—Colson's beautiful face floating in front of mine. The smile on his face is unexplainable. He's never looked so pure and happy as he does at this moment. Six months of torture can truly put into perspective that the little moments are what life is all about. Being with those who love, adore, and cherish your presence. I grab his face in my hands, pulling him to mine, and kiss his lips as if it's my last supper. Millions of tiny bubbles form around us, clouding my vision. Everett's and Dean's bodies come into view, both of them having jumped in beside us, making us break away from our kiss.

Breaking the surface, the sound of my laughter echoes through the night, a sound I'm not familiar with. Splashes of water hit my face as all three guys emerge from the surface, each one shaking out their hair. I squint my eyes, blocking my face from the water droplets before strong hands grab my chest below my breasts and push me to the side of the pool.

"I told you I could swim." Colson's voice is in my ear, his cool lips brushing the sensitive spot on my ear. I let out another laugh, tilting my head back against the edge of the pool.

"What's so funny?" he says to me, his hand wrapping around my throat and pulling my face to his.

"We're in the shallow end. This doesn't prove you can swim," I say to him. Everett and Dean make their way over to the side of the pool, joining our conversation.

"She's right, mate," Dean says, spitting water on the back of Colson's head. Everett swims up beside me, resting his back against the edge of the pool and resting his arms against the cold concrete.

"Fine then, I'll show you all. I can swim." Colson lets me go, the sudden absence of him makes me feel cold. Colson wades over to the deep end and takes a deep breath before submerging himself underneath the water.

"This ought to be good," Dean whispers to me as he joins my other side, mimicking Everett's posture as he, too, rests his arms across the concrete. A moment goes by, several bubbles float to the surface, but Colson remains underneath. More and more bubbles emerge, and my heart rate picks up as Colson has yet to break the surface.

"Colson?" I yell. Still nothing.

"Fuck," Dean says, as he dives down, swimming beneath the surface until I can see he's reached Colson's shadow. The pair of them push off the bottom of the pool, their bodies finally coming up for air. However, Colson isn't moving, his head hunched over as Dean swims the two of them back to the edge. I meet him halfway, grabbing Colson's face and lifting him to mine.

"Colson?!" I yell, his eyes snapping open as he spits water in my face. Coughing and sputtering, I wipe the water from my eyes.

"See, I told you I could swim," he jokes. He dips his head in the water again before whipping it back, his long blond hair causing a fan of water droplets to create a perfect circle above him.

"You jerk! That doesn't prove you can swim. Dean still saved you. All it proved is you can hold your breath." I push water onto his face, his bright white smile making it hard to be mad at him. Dean and Everett look less than amused as Dean puts his hand on top of Colson's head, dunking him in.

I swim back to the edge of the pool where Everett looks as chill as ever, resting his body against the side. I lean against his chest, his warm body inviting as he wraps his long arms around me. We both watch as Dean and Colson wrestle one another in the water as if the past ten months never happened. I lean my head against the crook of Everett's neck and close my eyes. The sounds of the night become clearer. The trees are blowing in the wind, the insects are chirping, and the sound of the guys splashing in the water has my heart feeling at peace.

"I love you, Everett," I whisper to him. His lips find the side of my face and he kisses me so tenderly, so softly, I never want this moment to end. If this is a dream, I want to stay here. Forever and always.

"I love you too, baby girl."

"I love you more." I open my eyes and see Colson swimming towards us.

"But we all know who you love the most." Dean grabs my waist as he speaks and pulls me into his body, my legs wrapping around his toned abdomen. "Tell them, love."

"You know I love all three of you the same," I giggle out, Dean now spinning us around in the shallow water. I lean forward, kissing him on the lips, and his hands tighten on my waist.

"What do you say you show us just how much you love us all?" Dean's voice is a shallow whisper, full of lust and desire.

CHAPTER 38

SLOAN

Everett is already behind me, his hard chest pressing close to my back as the familiar bulge in his boxers is now pressing against my back. His hand begins on my stomach, grabbing the hem of my shirt I'm still wearing, and pulls the fabric free from my skin. Tossing the shirt to the edge of the pool, a loud splat echoes through the backyard as Everett makes quick work of my bra. He unfastens my straps with quick fingers, and my breasts fall from my bra, submerging them in the water. I let out a soft moan, the water feeling so inviting to my naked skin. I release Dean's waist so I can begin stepping out of my leggings, Everett helping me as the fabric is so tight to my wet skin. Once freed, my skin is set on fire as a mouth covers my pussy, a tongue darting out and licking between my lips in one deep motion.

Looking down, I see Colson is beneath me, his face

distorted from the ripples in the water, but he's there, his tongue making me jerk and flinch with every flick against my clit.

"Holy fuck," I moan out, my head falling back and hitting Everett's shoulder as he holds me upright, as Colson works me over from beneath the water. Firm hands begin squeezing both of my breasts, twisting and pinching my nipples enough to sting. The pain of the pinching mixed with the pleasure between my legs is intoxicating.

"That a girl," Dean's gravelly voice is in my ear, his tongue licking that spot just behind my ear, giving me goosebumps. Just then Colson's mouth is gone, the sudden loss of sensation quickly cooling my body from an inferno to an ice bath.

"Wh-what? No, don't stop," I moan out. A chuckle combines with Colson's voice.

"I needed to come up for a breath, my dear. Here, let's go to the steps." Everett and Dean practically carry me to the steps, as Colson follows behind. Dean grabs underneath my arms and sits me on the top step. Colson grabs my ankles, pulling my ass to the edge of the step and spreading my legs wide for him. Staring down at Colson, he gives me a wicked smile, licking his lips before he begins feasting on my pussy once again. His warm mouth and tongue are the perfect contrast to the cooler water temperature, and I lean my head back.

Water beside me moves in quick motions as Dean exits the pool, my eyes opening to see him standing above me. I open my mouth in invitation to him, my tongue darting out as he kneels down, pulling his already erect cock from his boxers. As if we are remaking the Spiderman movie, but in a slightly different way, he inserts his cock slowly down my throat, his head hitting the back of my throat as I swallow him deeper.

"Fuckkkkk," he moans out. I hum around his length, and he twitches inside me. Pulling out and sliding back down my throat, he repeats this motion, setting a rhythm. My whole body ignites as Everett begins massaging my breasts once again. My nipples harden as the cold wind blows across my exposed chest. Colson's mouth leaves my needy pussy once again. He inhales a deep breath as he comes up for air.

"Flip her over, mate, I need to be inside this pussy now," Colson says to Dean, as he grabs my waist and flips me around so I'm now facing Dean, his hand stroking his cock as he lines himself back up with my mouth. I open wide, drool dripping down my chin as he fills me up. A loud smack echoes in the air as Colson's hand lands on my ass—a muffled shriek leaves my mouth, but I embrace the sting.

"So, fucking beautiful," Colson whispers, the head of his cock sliding up and down my entrance, and I lean back towards him, needing him to be inside me.

"Such a needy little thing, aren't you, sweetheart?"

I groan, my need for him growing as he continues to tease my entrance. Just then, warmth fills my pussy so slowly and deliciously, my knees shudder against the stairs. Colson moans as he fully inserts his cock, his front pressed firmly against my ass as he slides his hands down the length of my back. Pulling out completely, he lines himself up again, pushing harder this time until he's fully seated. I groan, the feeling of being utterly full making me see stars.

"I'm not sure I can wait much longer, mate," Everett's voice comes from behind me just as Colson pulls out of me again. Empty, I feel so empty, as the shifting water swirls around me again.

"Atta girl," I hear Everett, his fingers wrapping around my hips so painfully tight I'll surely have bruises. Without warning, Everett slams into me, pushing my body so hard I gag on Dean's cock as he hits the back of my throat.

"For fuck's sake, mate, careful," Dean says over my shoulder, his fingers threading through my hair as he pulls himself out of my mouth. I gasp and inhale deep breaths as Everett continues to pound relentlessly into me, his fingers digging into my skin. I grab the edge of the pool, my knuckles turning white with how hard I'm holding on.

"Oh, God!" I yell, the familiar feeling of ecstasy growing in my stomach. I'm so close. I match Everett's thrust with the sound of our skin slapping as water splashes between us. Just when I'm about to explode with pleasure, Everett pulls out.

"Wh-what? No, don't stop!" I scream, turning my head just in time to see Dean thrust his cock inside me. If I wasn't seeing stars already, I certainly am now. My three guys line up behind me, each taking turns as they thrust over and over again, my orgasm reaching the precipice just for it to be taken from me while the guys change positions. I want to scream in frustration each time, but I'm quickly silenced when I'm instantly filled once again.

"She's so close boys, every fucking time." A devilish laugh chuckles from behind me just as my body tightens once more, the sensation stolen from me as I'm left empty.

"Fuckkkk, please," I whine, my head falling towards the water as my climax disappears slowly. Suddenly, a hand is wrapped around my throat, my head being pulled back in a painfully awkward position.

"You'll cum when we say you cum, love." Everett's dark voice is by my ear, his words giving me shivers as he shoves his cock in completely. My breathing picks up as he holds my neck back, squeezing my throat just enough that it's becoming hard to breathe. Everett continues his rhythm, the thrusts becoming harder and harder as his speed picks up.

"You ready for me, love?" he whispers in my ear, my vision going spotted as I struggle for a breath. I can't respond to him; I can't move at all. I'm chasing my orgasm as quickly as I can in fear of him leaving me once more. His body is lying against my back as his abdomen flexes against me. He's close too. I can feel him twitching inside me. Without warning, I'm hit by a volcanic eruption that starts from my core and bleeds through my entire being. A wave of pleasure that feels like an out-of-body experience. I'm floating and drowning at the same time. I'm silent yet screaming my release as Everett pulls away from me, Dean quickly taking his place and continuing his rhythm.

I have no time to come down. I remain in the harmonious paradise as Dean thrusts faster and faster and another orgasm crests within me. A continuous roller coaster, a tsunami of endless waves, crashing over me as I'm hit with what can only be described as heaven on earth. I've lost all sense of hearing as I see Dean move to my front, but the feeling of being full remains. I glance over my shoulder to see Colson is now thrusting his cock in and out, my body screaming between orgasms. Could a girl die from too many orgasms? Asking for a friend because at this moment I don't know when one orgasm starts and the next ends.

"Look at me, love—you're doing so well." Dean's steel-gray eyes are locked on mine as he cups his hands around my face, holding me firm. My whole body is trembling, shaking in pleasure, my climax reaching an all-time high. I scream my release, the feeling of Colson's pace slowing as I hear a deep groan from behind me. His hands sliding up my back and wrapping around my front to my breasts. He holds me tight to his warm body. The only sound I can hear now is the four of us breathing, inhaling deep breaths as my guys continue to hold me up. I'd surely drown if they let me go.

My body comes crashing down from my cloud of paradise, adrenaline slowing down as my body feels limp.

"Such a good girl," I hear Everett say, his voice deep and full of lust as he continues breathing heavily.

"Come on, let's get her inside." That's the last thing I hear before my vision goes dark. I couldn't even tell you who said that.

I awake in a warm bed, the lights dark, and my naked body wrapped in the silkiest of silk sheets. Peeling my eyes open, I see I'm not alone. Everett, Dean, and Colson are all here with me. Their naked bodies sprawled out on either side of me. The room has a dim glow, candles are lit all across Colson's dresser, illuminating the room just enough to make out each one of their faces.

I smile. I don't wake them, I just lay there between my guys, safe, full, and so fucking happy. I never thought I'd get a happily ever after, and to be honest, we have a long life ahead of us, but this, this is a life I've only ever dreamt of.

Going back to that day at the café, I wouldn't change a single moment in my life. Everything that happened was supposed to happen in the exact way it did. I was meant to be taken, brought to the Fortress, taken again, and everything in between. As much pain and trauma as the four of us have endured, I feel as though I speak for all of us when I say I wouldn't change a thing. Everything has led me to who I am today, I'm Sloan, I'm a Shadow, and I'm by far the luckiest fucking girl in this entire world.

"Keep thinking that hard, you'll make wrinkles in the pretty forehead of yours," Colson whispers beside me. Turning to see his eyes are still closed, but he's smiling that perfect smile that makes my stomach flutter with butterflies. I roll towards him, cuddling into his chest as I gaze up at his face.

"I was just thinking how lucky I am to be with you three," I whisper back to him, leaning in and kissing the tip of his nose. Opening his eyes, he returns the gesture, kissing the tip of my nose.

"No, my dear, it's us who are the lucky ones. You may think we've saved you but, in all seriousness, you've saved us." A dip in the bed behind me has me turning my head over my shoulder. Everett turns towards me, wrapping his arm around my stomach and pulling himself tight to my back.

"You saved us from a life of numbness. I'm convinced you were put in our path to open our eyes and allow us to crawl from the depths of hell into the arms of an angel." His lips brush against my neck, warm breath tingling chills throughout my body.

"Without you, baby girl, the three of us would have fallen victim to a life wiped clean of all emotion. Walking through life as robots doing as we're told, not knowing what love could be, what it could look like, or what it truly felt like. You think we saved you from a life of loveless existence? No, my dear, you've shown us what it's like to live outside the shadows. The light feels so much better than the abyss of darkness. You've awakened our hearts and brought us back to life," Dean says from behind Colson.

"We've saved each other, love triumphs all," I say to the three of them, my voice a soft whisper as the four of us remain as one.

EPILOGUE

SLOAN

"Where almost here," I say over my shoulder to Arno, who looks all types of annoyed with my antics as he sits cramped in the back seat of my new Mercedes GLC. Once we returned home, I waited to open Shem's envelope. I'm not sure why, I just felt as though I needed to wait. After roughly three weeks, the guys convinced me to open it and, to my surprise, it was Shem's fortune in its entirety. Four and half million dollars and five properties, including the one my guys were prisoners at. I demolished that compound the moment I could. A true rag to riches story if you ask me. However, I took a majority of the money and put it towards rehabilitation centers for those who have been abused and or sexually assaulted. We currently have twenty-two centers and are growing.

When I told the guys this was the vehicle I

wanted, they tried everything in their power to get me to change my mind. They wanted me to get something slicker, more sport-like, but for me this was perfect. I've been a Shadow now for roughly three weeks, and I couldn't be more convinced this is what I was put on this earth to do. Eliminating the evils of this world is something I never knew I would excel at. I've been on more jobs these past few weeks than anyone else, and I can't see myself slowing down. The guys have tried their best to pull me back a bit, but I enjoy this work and doing something that betters the innocent people of this world is what keeps me going. The younger me wouldn't believe who we've become today, and that makes me smile the most.

"I don't even know where here is, little one. Plus, I'm getting hungry, so this needs to be sped up just a bit quicker," Arno whines again from the back. Turning around to look at him, I give him a smile.

"You're always hungry so that's not new, and trust me, you'll like where I'm taking you." Arno scoffs from the back seat as he leans back and tosses his head against the headrest.

"Listen, mate, I'll get you a Happy Meal when we're through. How does that sound?" Colson jokes as he turns on the blinker, turning down a gravel road.

"As long as I get a milkshake to go with it," Arno adds under his breath. Laughing, I look down at my phone and check the GPS.

"We're about two minutes away. I think you'll

survive a moment longer."

"I beg to differ," the big grump pouts some more just as we pull to a stop at a remote building that's labeled *Bright Paths Home for Women and Children.* Pulling to the gate, Colson rolls down his window, and I show him my phone that lists the eight-digit code to open the gate. I catch a glimpse of Arno in the backseat, his expression quickly going from annoyed to curious as he reads the sign above the gate.

After I heard Arno talking with someone about finding Willow, I took Colson to see one of the many counselors at headquarters. We spoke about his journal and how he listed a woman named Willow he had saved from a warehouse. This particular job stuck with him, especially with Willow and how calm she was with the whole situation she had been thrown into. Victims are always brought to rehabilitation centers owned and operated by The Shadows to ensure they receive the care they need before they reenter society.

When I brought up Willow to Mrs. Jackie, she wasn't too happy that I knew anything about one of the victims. Shadows are under no circumstance allowed to communicate or know about the victims in any way. However, after reading Colson's diary, I couldn't hide my knowledge of how I knew about her. Colson got into some trouble as well for taking his journal home, but it didn't take too much finesse after I expressed my concern for Willow and how she could be someone of high importance to Arno.

After agreeing to help us hunt down Willow, it took some time, but we finally found her whereabouts at one of the rehabilitation centers. Mrs. Jackie agreed to allow us to see her; however, she would need to speak with Willow first and see if she was even willing to see us or Arno. According to Mrs. Jackie, there was no hesitation on Willow's part, the first mention of Arno, and she instantly demanded to be brought to him.

The moment Mrs. Jackie called me and told me Willow wanted to see Arno as soon as possible, Colson and I practically kidnapped Arno and brought him here. This rehabilitation center is roughly two hours from the headquarters, this one being the closest by far. The Shadows own twelve rehabilitation centers located all around the world. From the United States all the way to Mongolia. It's truly fascinating and incredible the measures the organization takes to ensure the overall health and well-being of the victims we save. Another reason I love this job more and more.

We pull through the gates, rounding the driveway until we pull up to a long flight of stairs that lead to a beautiful stone facility that reminds me of a university. The long staircase is lined with gorgeous stone flowerpots that hold greenery that extends the length of the pots. The place is incredibly well kept, especially since it's away from any town or city. As grand as this place is, it brings a cozy feeling.

The front door opens, and Mrs. Jackie makes her

way down the stairs, meeting me with a hug at our car.

"So good to see you again, my dear," she says in her warm, inviting voice.

"Mrs. Jackie? What are you doing here?" Arno says from behind me. He emerges from the back seat, his eyebrows pinched so hard together in confusion it's hard to keep my smile hidden. Mrs. Jackie doesn't answer him, she just gives him a bright smile as she walks up to him and wraps her delicate arms around the big man. He leans down to her level, making it easier for her to hug him. She's a small lady, barely five foot and pushing seventy, but you wouldn't know her age just by looking at her. She's kept herself in phenomenal shape. I have this theory that she was once a Shadow as well before she retired, but instead of stopping her work altogether, she's developed the rehabilitation centers for the women and children.

I hope to be her one day, forever saving the innocent from staying victims to the evils of this world. Arno looks up at me, his expression lost in thought and more confused by the minute.

Mrs. Jackie releases Arno, standing up and grabbing his hand before leading him up the long stairs, Colson and I following behind. Reaching the top of the stairs, she stops and turns to face Arno.

"I have someone that's quite literally dying to see you." With that, the front door creaks open, all our gazes turning to face it. The moment the door fully opens, the silence that surrounds us is deafening.

Willow, a dark-haired, slender woman, steps outside, the sun beaming off her delicate face. Green eyes light up at the sight of the man standing in front of her, her plump lips instantly stretching across her face as a tear begins sliding down her cheek.

"Arno," Willow whispers, her voice so small, so angelic my heart beats faster at the sight of her. My hand finds Colson's as we thread our fingers together, and I squeeze his tight. I look up to see Arno's face is in utter shock. The once hardened brute of a man has now transformed into a small child. His eyebrows are raised so high as his mouth falls parted slightly, his eyes rapidly filling with tears as his breathing has picked up. She's the one. Finally found his happily ever after. A tragic love story that's been transformed into the best and happiest ending no person could ever write. My heart aches as I watch these two fall in love all over again in front of me.

Willow rushes from where she stands, her body colliding with his as he lifts her into his arms, her legs wrapping around his waist as she sobs into his neck.

"Willow," Arno whispers into her hair, the pair falling to the ground, embracing one another in what must feel like a dream. I look over my shoulder at Colson, his smile matching mine.

"I love you, Colson."

"I love you too, baby girl. Always and forever."

The End.

TO MY READERS:

We made it! We've come to the end of Sloan's long and eventful journey! This last book, for me, was by far the most fun to write. We had a lot of cleaning up to do. I want to thank everyone who made it to the end and enjoyed this roller coaster of a ride. This trilogy was my first jump into the writing community and I'm so glad I took the plunge back in 2020.

I want to thank my designer and cover creator, Abigail, who has worked with me through this whole trilogy. She made my ideas and images come to life and couldn't be happier with the outcome. To my editor, Maddi, thank you for helping transform my style so it flows and reads fluently. I can't wait to work with you both very soon!

Again, thank you to my readers for you I would not be where I am today.

Much love to you all.

ABOUT THE AUTHOR

Rebecca is a newly published author who lives in North Carolina with her husband, two kids, and four-legged friend. You will usually find her escaping into her writing where her deepest and darkest thoughts are created for others to enjoy. When she is not writing she is either exercising, listening to audio-books, playing with her kids, watching true crime documentaries or zoning out while thinking of all the ways to torture her characters. As most of us authors nowadays say, check trigger warnings before diving in. Thank you for being here!

Learn more about Rebecca Hamby at rebeccahambyauthor.com. Join her newsletter to receive updates, teasers, giveaways, and special deals!

www.ingramcontent.com/pod-product-compliance
Lightning Source LLC
Chambersburg PA
CBHW071356150726
48000CB00001B/44